AF241332

Medical Comedy, "Making It"

Nathalie Schlager

Candles flicker as I open the door to our apartment, and Sandra walks slowly toward me wearing a sheer white negligee that clings to her well-developed breasts and slim hips. She puts her arms around me and we kiss. It is a long, long kiss. Her tongue slides between my lips, into my mouth, and she grew drops to the floor.

Sandra has faith that this ritual will eventually help me overcome the sexual problem that is caused by my condition and goes to great lengths attempting to have sex as often as humanly possible.

Neither one of us had our eyes closed when we married five years ago in 1998. We both had a lot of experience in the thirty-five years we were single and Sandra knew we may never have children, but the reality never hit her until this year when she turned forty. She also understood my condition made it difficult for me to keep a job, that's why we moved into the least expensive place Brooklyn, her mother's house.

I have lived this way for many years and have seen almost every sex professional and medical doctor listed in the yellow pages, but none of them or their medicines help me.

Sandra has been very understanding about everything and when she looks at me with those sweet, sincere, solemn eyes of hers and tips her head to the side, like a trusting, little cocker spaniel puppy, I realize how very lucky I am to have her.

Sandra is a beautiful person outside as well inside. She has this endless, dark brown hair and large, black, almond-shaped eyes with fantastic long lashes. She reminds me a little of Julia Roberts, but she's barely five feet tall and a little sensitive about her height, so she wears these very, very high heels that give her a taller appearance.

Sandra makes me feel loved, something I never had from my parents because they both died in a car crash when I was three.

My mother's sister Marie and her husband raised me with their son Sylvester. Marie tried to be a good mother to us but she just didn't want it bad enough. She loved the bottle more than she loved us.

Sylvester died when he was twenty from the Mongolian Flu. It hurt me to lose him because we were like brothers. We even looked like brothers, thin and dark with curly black hair. People told us we looked like Dean Martin and should be in the movies but I may not have found Sandra if I was a movie star.

Although I am out of work, Sandra has a great job working in a bank. Her mother, Vera, really enjoys her work, too. She works on me. Vera and I have this love/hate relationship. I love her cooking and she hates my being broke.

I found out it is not good living too close to your mother-in-law, especially if her husband is dead because then there is only one man around to punish.

Vera knows all about our sex life. She hears everything we say since our walls have ears, hers! When Sandra and I discuss things Vera says we fought. She says the bathroom pipes tell her every time I have my problem.

Today, after such an event, ma bell amia (my beautiful one) walked into our apartment and announced,

"From my ceiling, a drip is coming."

When I didn't respond she thought I didn't hear, so she asked,

"You hear my mouth, Tony?"

"Sure Mama, I hear your mouth. Your mouth is easy to hear, for miles and miles everyone--"

"Mama, we already called the plumber," Sandra said, but Mama wasn't happy.

"Tony, always the bathroom pipes you clog! Already, two trips to Paris for my plumber I paid!"

I sat quietly, looked at my wonderful wife, and thought about my mother-in-law's delicious cooking, but this was one of those days when I could not keep silent.

"I love you Mama, but I especially love the way you don't knock on our door when you come to visit."

"Permission I should get? Maybe a whole ceremony you need? Maybe before I come in the shoes should come off, too?"

Sandra kissed her mother on the cheek.

"Mama, don't be upset. We just need a little privacy." "Before I am leaving, Tony, I want you should know, down the street, the Mobil gas station is. A toilet has, privacy it has, and welcome you should feel clogging their pipes!"

Vera started to leave but pearls of wisdom continued to run from her mouth.

"My wonderful son Milton, a brilliant doctor he is. You should see."

"I'm not going to anyone in the family!"

"Already he knows the problem you have."

"My condition is a private matter!" I yelled.

"Only the family I tell."

"Oh, so all Brooklyn knows."

"Go, see my Milton."

"He won't be able to help me. I've already seen a doctor like him."

"Like my son? Never! From all over to him they come. A specialist with hands of gold and such a trained finger! You know what it costs to educate such a finger?"

Vera opened the door and as her mother's chubby body waddled down the stairs, she called to me.

"Go visit the finger, for you it would be free from charge." Sandra closed the door and continued where her mother left off.

"She's right Tony; it wouldn't hurt to see my brother. All your doctors and medicines haven't helped you. You've tried everything on the market." She opened the kitchen cabinets.

"Look! We have our pharmacy but nothing works." She put her arms around me.

"Tony, I love you but our marriage needs help. You've got to get better so you can hold down a job. And I need you to hold me and make love to me and make a baby with me. I'm not getting younger. My biological clock is ticking away!"

"You know I want us to have sex together. It is hell never being able to enjoy that part of life!"

"I'm not blaming you, Tony." Sandra held me tight. I kissed her hair, her brow, and her lips."

"Sandra, you knew before we married that I wasn't able to have sex. Did you think some miracle would change me?"

"I believe in miracles. We have to keep trying, Tony. Somewhere there is a doctor who can help us."

"When we married you only wanted me."

"I still want you Tony, but a baby would be part of both of us so I would have more of you to love."

"We could try in vitro or artificial insemination."

"No Tony. I need to find out if there is the slightest possibility that we can make a baby ourselves before we attempt those other things."

I nervously walked around. At this point, I felt our marriage could go down the drain. I looked at my adorable wife sitting there so unhappy.

"OK, make an appointment with your brother Milton, thee *rear* admiral."

It is now two weeks that I'm in Gramercy Hospital, in New York City. Thanks to my brother-in-law, Milton. I have been pinched, probed, and punctured with everything doctors can legally use. I've had my blood drained so many times I look like a porcupine with his needles pulled out. I can't lie down, sit up, or stand without pain in my ass. Hour after hour, day by day, I wait and worry about the results of my tests. At night, after work, Sandra sits and worries with me.

Early this morning Milton came in to tell me I was being moved from my semi-private room to a private room with a private nurse called Betty.

"I don't want to be moved! I can't afford it. We don't have that kind of coverage from Sandra's insurance at work."

"It's all taken care of. Don't' worry about the cost," Milton tells me.

After a few days in my new room, I noticed a man standing outside my door all day and a different one at night, but no one will tell me why he is there.

I've been put on a strict diet, and no friends are allowed to visit me, only the immediate family. The doctors insist I stay in bed. I'm not even allowed to walk to the bathroom, so I have to use a bedpan labeled, 'high priority'.

When I question Milton, he says I'm not dangerously ill, but Sandra doesn't believe him and is very unhappy. My mother-in-law seems very, very happy, this frightens me.

Today I was escorted downstairs for more tests. A tall, six-foot female nurse lifted me, then rolled me over onto my stomach, raised my hospital gown, and came at me with that looked like the tube from a vacuum cleaner. As I yelled in fear, Milton walked in and assured me the test would be painless. He put on gloves, gave me a shot, and the nurse handed him the vacuum cleaner.

I clutched my fists as it went in. Instrument after instrument probed me until the injection wore off and I cried out in pain.

"I never hurt my patients, Tony. They may suffer a little but I never hurt them."

"Roto-Rooter would be less painful," I told him.

"Just relax, relax Tony. It may be a little uncomfortable now, but I'm almost at the root of the problem," Suddenly he was finished. He picked up what he said was my specimen, and stared at it.

"This little thing is very, very interesting." He put it in a container and told me he was taking it directly to the lab.

"Tony, you're in the good hands. I have excellent doctors working with me but so far the answers we've come up with stymie us."

"It isn't anything serious is it Milton?"

"Don't worry," he assured me, "we will take care of whatever is wrong." He gave me a pat on the back and left me alone with the nurse who took me to my fancy cage, where Sandra greeted me with hugs and kisses.

"Tony, no one would tell me where you were. I was afraid something happened." She said with tears in her eyes.

Sandra cried very easily. She was like a bucket of water filled to the brim and waiting to be tipped. I held her close to me, wiped her tears, and lied to hear about coming home next week, as Vera walked in.

"So much trouble I had coming here."

"You could have called instead," I suggested.

"So, to everyone, you will complain how your mother-in-law doesn't visit?"

"It wouldn't be a complaint," I said as Vera sat and fanned herself.

Just then, Milton arrived and delivered his usual handshake and kisses. He said it would be a few more days before all the tests would be back, but we shouldn't worry.

"We see some stones that form in your stomach which are unusual in substance, but" the new medicines we are going to give you should help. Nothing is certain, but I want you to know we are working on it. "Then, with a smile and backward wave, he went out the door."

"What does he mean by unusual stones, Tony?"

"He doesn't sound like he knows anything yet."

Vera rose to leave. "Tony, maybe an evil curse your trouble is from."

"Since when have you believed in evil curses, Ma?"

"How long have you and my daughter been married?" Vera quickly disappeared out the door.

A few days later, Milton came in with two new doctors who did more tests. My nurse whispered to me, "These doctors are world renown. They were flown in from different parts of the world to study you." My nurse should never have told me this. Now I knew I was seriously ill!

Sandra and her mother came in after the tests, and Milton introduced them to the doctors. When Dr. Tong said he recently arrived here from China, Vera asked,

"In China, problems like Tony's you have?"

"There are a great many stomach problems in my country. Our people eat so much rice their stomachs become like the Great Wall of China. It isn't until they hear the American food that the walls come tumbling down."

I interrupted, "I want to know why so many doctors from all over the world are working on me? Do I have some new disease? Something none of you ever heard of before? Why don't you tell me what is going on?"

"You think maybe Tony can die? Maybe his insurance I should pay it up?"

Milton took Vera by the arm to the door, but she ran back into the room and pleaded,

"I'll be quite. I'll be good. Not a word, not a sound, not a breath will I take. See? The breathing it's stopped."

Bella, Bella, (beautiful, beautiful) I thought, how lucky can I get?

Sandra sat next to me on the bed as Milton tried to answer my questions.

"Tony, what we think you have is not dangerous or fatal, but very difficult to live with unless you have medical help. Your condition is a very, very unusual one. We will keep testing but we are running out of tests. Now, if your illness, your problem, is what it appears to be----it can be extremely advantageous to you."

"It's advantageous? That's ridiculous! This, this thing I have has caused me misery all my life! How can you possibly call it advantageous?" I yelled.

Dr. Tong stood up. "Let me try to explain. " There was complete silence. "Some people can create from their brain like, Einstein, Madame Curie, and Louis Pasteur. Other people are gifted with unusual abilities to do things with their bodies. Some can tie their bodies into knows, while others do magic with their body like Houdini. Now, Tony, you have an extraordinary way of producing unusual things from your body."

"What am I producing?"

Milton explained, "We can't say right now. These unusual things have to be studied further by our specialists.

You must also realize the three of you that you mustn't talk to anyone about anything we have discussed here today!"

"Why do we need to keep everything so secretive?" Sandra asked.

"For safety reasons."

"Safety reason?" We all chimed in and stared at Milton.

"This is all we can tell you now, but we must keep everything we talk about strictly between us. I must emphasize this because if what the other doctors and myself suspect is happening to you leaks out Toney, everyone will want something from you. Our government will justifiably grab you, never mind the foreign governments."

"It's Impazzito! (crazy) It's crazy, I yelled. I couldn't believe my ears."

"What are you talking about, Milton?" Sandra asked hysterically, "Why would our government grab Tony or anyone grabs him? Tony hasn't done anything wrong. We don't owe the government anything. We paid our taxes."

"And I paid my debt to society when I enlisted and served in the Marines. When President Regan needed us to stop the trouble in Grenada, in 1983, I was there! My family was very poor and hardworking and we had no connections with the Mafia! I never even had a Godfather!" I was really pissed!

"Tony, Tony, take it easy." Milton put his arm around me. "I'm only telling you what I've been told to say by my superiors. If I could tell you more I would."

"Milton, you're more than my doctor. We are family. I trust you. You wouldn't lie to me, would you?"

"Never! I would never lie to you, Tony. Now I have to go. I have an operation to prepare for." He gave Sandra a much-needed hug and left with the other two doctors.

"My son Milton, I don't know, since he doesn't make it when he talks. I am so worried about my Milton."

Sandra stared at her mother. "Mother, I can't understand you. You are visiting my husband in the hospital, who is suffering from we don't know what, and all you can worry about is Milton!"

"Because my son doesn't sound normal and he doesn't look with hair hanging down his back, and a red ribbon, yet. From the ex-wives, ex-mothers-in-law, ex-girlfriends, mixed up in the head he is!

Wife number one, the magician, made gelt (money) disappears. Wife number two, the witch, on her broomstick, flies to his Mercedes, and then both disappear.

Why people attract people, I never could understand, until one day, I saw a famous world doctor on television. Smells, he says, attract smells. Now I understand my Milton. From his work that smells, attracts strange people."

"Mother, I'm worried about Tony right now, not about smells attracting smells!"

"I know, I know, but I want you to both to escape from worry, so a true story about mine husband I will tell. The love of my life, in a restaurant, found me. There, a wonderful cook I was, but from onions, I smelled. One schmeck (smell) he would take and away I could not get. Me, so much he loved, and so much my body he needed. Such a romantic! With onions mine skin he would cover, then slowly he would taste, as his tongue would lick off."

Vera had me laughing. The thought of any man licking onions off Vera's little fat body made me hysterical, but I could tell Sandra was embarrassed.

"Mother, you're making up stories, and I think your son Milton is just like you! He's making up a story about Tony's sickness. Whoever heard of an advantageous sickness?"

"But Milton isn't the only doctor involved," I said. "They can't all be making up stories."

"Maybe a call I give my Machuga (crazy) son about the men in the little white coats coming. I think depressed in the head he is. You Tony, in the belly a depression you have." Sandra and I listened as Vera called Milton on my phone.

"I know Dr. Horwitz's office it is. Who else would be in his number? This is his mother calling." (silence) "An appointment to talk to my son I need? No appointment to be born he made. Two months late he was, from the onions they told me."

"Mother, you will drive Milton's secretary crazy!"

Vera continued. "For Milton's baby food, nursing milk, never appointments, everything on-demand it was. I'll tell you, easy it wasn't." (silence) "Hold? I don't want I should hold. Connect me to my son if your job you should want to keep!"

At that moment, Dr. Peck, a psychiatrist, came to my room and my mother-in-law was asked to leave.

"You want I should leave because too sexual for me you talk? Believe me, about sex I know."

"Mother!"

"Mine lust, mine passion, mine husband is killed. Right in the middle, doing it."

"Mother!"

"My son-in-law, lust and passion he can't die from. My daughter, without it she lives." Sandra went to the door.

"Mother, the door is open and waiting for you."

Vera finally left my room, but before Dr. Peck began I told him about the previous shrinks that never helped me. He explained his procedure could work because it would connect my brain to my stomach function and help my rectal process.

"Dr. Peck may be able to help you, Tony," Sandra said. "Maybe his way is different from the others."

I let the doctor proceed.

"Tony, you must concentrate more about what you're doing and when and where you do it."

This profound statement caused Sandra to question the doctor.

"How long did you say you've been in practice?"

He informed us he was a Harvard Medical School graduate and in practice for four years. These made us more confident that he had the latest medical knowledge, so I paid attention as he continued.

"Your problem began way back. We must retreat to the security of your childhood, before your childhood, before you were conceived, and when you were only a thought."

Sandra looked at me, and I looked at her.

"Now I am going to question you about your sex life, so just answer as honestly as possible.

Do you ejaculate before you need to go to the bathroom?"

"The need to go to the bathroom stops me from ejaculating."

"If you wait and don't go to the bathroom, will you eventually ejaculate?"

"No. And I will make a terrible mess in the bed."

Dr. Peck looked very pleased with himself as he wrote my answers.

"So, your penis doesn't go up, consequently, it doesn't fall down. That's very interesting."

"Tony takes Viagra with his breakfast, lunch, and dinner. It helps grow hair on his head, and he gets full of pep, but not between his legs."

"Interesting. Now, about your childhood, Tony, your childhood on the potty, was your mother obsessive-compulsive concerning your toilet training?"

"I really don't remember."

"When you were on the potty, did your mother stay with you?" "I don't recall."

"Did she close the bathroom door and leave you alone on the potty? And if she did, was this loneliness upsetting to you?"

I couldn't believe this guy, but he said we only had a few more questions so I gave him the benefit of my doubts.

"Were you kept on the potty for hours until you did it? Were you ever allowed to get off the potty if you didn't do it? Now this last question is very, very important. Listen carefully, and don't let it upset you. Did your mother die while you were on the potty?"

I had it! I took my adult potty and threw it at Dr. Peck's pecker. He swore and jumped as I hit my mark! The Harvard impazzito (crazy) ran out yelling and holding his organ. It was music to my ears.

My nurse tucked me under the covers and told Sandra to leave. As I lay there alone, I thought to myself, too bad my potty wasn't full.

The days passed very slowly, and the longer they kept me in the hospital the more certain I became that there wasn't much hope for me.

Two more weeks passed, then, very early one bleak morning, I woke up to find Dr. Tong and Dr. Sinclair staring down at me.

"Were you studying how I sleep?" They tapped my body with their little metal, rubber- tipped instruments and smiled.

"Am I normal?"

They looked at each other.

"I understand that there could be something unusual in my body. Did you learn any more about this?"

They looked at each other as if questioning whether to answer me. Finally, Dr. Sinclair replied in his impeccable English accent.

"We are studying your breathing. It seems your snoring is rather unique. We hear one long, one short, two short, one long. You may be sending signals. It could be a code."

"A code? Whoever heard of snoring in code?"

"Oh, yes! Quite definitely! It is an important scientific study in England."

"What does my nose have to do with my sex problem? I don't get the picture."

"Well, they are both projectiles, but we will leave it up to Dr. Milton to paint the final picture."

As they left, I reflected on the word 'final'. It sounded too much like a death sentence. I called my nurse.

"I want to go home! I am sick of these tests on my body and mind. I am leaving!" My nurse immediately called Milton.

"I don't want to be a guinea pig any longer," I told my brother-in-law. "I'm going home."

Milton sat down and cleared his throat. "Look, I know it's difficult."

"Difficult? You don't know half of it. I am more uncomfortable now than I was at home! My ass is sore from this bed, the damn needles, and the bedpan! Some guy stands outside my door like a guard. I feel like a prisoner. I am a prisoner! You're not helping me, Milton. I am leaving here today!" I started to get off the bed when Sandra and Vera burst into my room.

"Running after us, he was." Vera cried breathlessly. Sandra highly excited and carrying her heels sank into a chair.

"This guy was following us! He came over to us as soon as we came into the parking lot. He kept taking our pictures and asking questions. He followed us right into the hospital. We had to run to get away from him."

"It sounds like the paparazzi (reporters)."

"New York Daily News, he tells us."

"He knew my name was Sandra Costello, and he kept asking strange questions."

"What did he ask you?"

"What do you think about what's happened to your husband? Are you happy about his unusual ability? Do you think fame and fortune will change you? What caused this miracle in your husband's body?' He called it a miracle, Tony!"

"When my picture he took, I told him, my name is Vera Horwitz, and I'm the Mother-in-law of the miracle. From my chicken soup, the miracle was born."

"Where is that reporter now?" Milton asked.

In unison, they pointed to the hall.

"He followed us to this room!"

Milton opened the door to a bright flash of light as the reporter snapped his picture.

The guard outside the door grabbed him as Milton asked angrily.

"Who sent you? Who gave you information about what's happening here?"

"We don't divulge our sources. This is a great story. Is Tony Costello your brother-in-law?"

I could see from my bed the little red-haired reporter was getting ready to take my picture, but as the guard fought to grab the camera, it crashed to the floor.

"You must destroy those pictures!" Milton yelled.

"Are you crazy? I was told this is the greatest story since we landed on the moon!" He bent down and picked up what was left of his camera. The guard held him as he wrote in his little notebook. "I hope I have your name spelled correctly, Dr. Horwitz. We like to keep the facts in order. Just what did you find that has to be kept such a secret? I've been told lots of things but I'd like it straight from the horse's mouth."

"Get out of here! What's happening in this hospital is not for the public to know! Guard! Orderly! Get this reporter out of this hospital!" Milton yelled.

As they took him away, all the visitors, patients, and nurses who heard the commotion peered at me through the doorway. Milton came into my room and carefully shut the door.

"I knew we couldn't keep this a secret for long. I wanted more time to make sure we were right in our diagnosis but once the reporters' start---."

"Maybe for obituary column he writes."

"Mother, what is your tongue saying?" Sandra asked.

"I think you have that foot-in-mouth disease, Mother!" Milton exclaimed as Vera pouted.

"What did the reporter mean when he asked my wife about my "fame and fortune, Milton"?

"A joke they play." Vera answered.

"Why would the Daily News want a story about me? Damn it, Milton, tell me!"

"I don't know how this information leaked out. It hasn't even been fully confirmed. I'm waiting to hear the other doctors' final reports and until that time, I have no authority to say anything. I'm sorry. I really am sorry but I can't tell any of you about what is going on."

"Tell us off the record, Milton. We are family!" I yelled as he went out the door.

A few days later, Milton came to my room.

"So?" I asked.

"Soon." Milton said.

"How soon?" Sandra questioned.

"Dr. Tong and Dr. Sinclair will be here any minute."

"The final reports they will have?" Vera asked.

"Yes. This is the day we've been waiting for."

We sat quietly, nervously staring at each other until the doctors came in.

"Dr. Milton, would you please come out to the corridor?" Milton left, closing my door tightly behind him.

Vera went to the door and pressed her ear against it. "It's not kosher (right). Nothing can I hear. I think I'll give a look." She opened the door a crack.

"What's happening?" I asked.

"Three shtarkers give a gezunt dir in pupik."

"What does that mean?" I nervously asked.

"It's nothing to be upset about, Tony. It only means three strong men are blessing your belly button." Sandra explained.

I became more nervous from this remark because I interpreted it as meaning they were giving me my last rites! I didn't want Sandra to go on a crying jag, so I kept it to myself.

Finally, Milton, all smiles, came back into my room. "We have the conclusive test results. What we all suspected is true!"

I tried to control my emotions as Milton paced up and down.

"Here's the picture, but I have to talk softly so no one hears. Walls have ears, so I'll talk very, very softly. Pull your chairs closer."

Sandra and Vera pulled their chairs close to Milton as I laid my head fiat on my pillow and stared at the ceiling.

"Before I say anything, you three, Tony, Sandra, and especially you Mother, must promise me you will not tell anyone about what I am about to say." Sandra exploded.

"Stop it, Milton! You sound paranoid! Just tell us the true story. The walls only have ears in Mother's house."

"Okay, here it is." Milton sat down. "All the doctors on this case, the specialists, the metallurgist---"

"What is a metallurgist?" Sandra questioned.

"A metallurgist practices the science and procedures of extracting metal from their ores. He is the scientist with all this particular knowledge that we need since he studies metals."

"From Tony's rectal he's looking for metal?" Vera asked.

Milton gave his mother a look and pointed to the door. She immediately covered her mouth with her hand, and Milton continued.

"All the doctors and all the specialists concur." Milton smiled happily, "Tony, you are making medical history!"

I couldn't believe what I heard. I still wasn't sure I understood as Sandra lashed out angrily at her brother.

"We came here for you, to make my husband better! Not for you to use him to make medical history so you can become famous! You've used him as a guinea pig for your own selfish reasons, and to think, I trusted you!" Sandra sobbed hysterically.

"Now, look what you've done to your sister!" I started to get out of bed and go over to her, but Milton held me back.

"One day, you will thank me for this. I know it's been tough for all of you. Tony's suffered through a lot of pain from tests, endless hours under surveillance, separation from Sandra, and general unhappiness for over a month, but it is worth everything you've gone through! Your medical problem, Tony, can be very, very beneficial to you financially."

"Milton, so brilliant you were. To your mind, what is happening?" Vera bent over and kissed her son on his head.

"Mother, why do you always take your son's side? Don't you realize what he is doing? He expects us to believe that my husband's problem, which stops him from having sex, holding a job, and living normally, is beneficial to us, but I think something is going on with you, Milton and these specialists, and this hospital! It sounds like a scam that will make the headlines and put us all in jail! Maybe there's something wrong with your hospital's accounting books, so you're looking to get some revenue through devious methods."

Milton put his arm around Sandra and calmly replied.

"I wouldn't do anything to hurt you or Tony, Sandra, and certainly not Mother. I wouldn't lie, and tests don't lie."

"You just don't understand, Milton. We don't want to benefit from Tony being sick. We don't want to have a sickness that makes us money. I just want a simple life with my husband." Sandra replied.

"A life with a simpleton my daughter wants. Money, a nice house, a car, who needs such things? To Paris, my plumber, I should keep sending."

"Listen, just listen," Milton pleaded. "We originally thought Tony was just passing stones, but they are not ordinary stones!"

I figured Milton just didn't have the guts to tell me how sick I was, but then he said, "There is nothing, nothing in your body that is dangerous, and you will have even fewer problems as long as we take care of you. We now know what you produce, but there is no answer to why you have this ability. You, Tony, are a phenomenon, a once in a lifetime phenomenon."

We were all speechless. We stared at each other, not quite knowing what to say or what to think.

"I have the greatest team of doctors and scientists from all over the world working on your case, but the most difficult thing to do is to keep it hush-hush."

"Hush-hush?" I asked.

"Yes," Milton said. "It must be kept as a secret!"

"Why? Why must we keep my sickness a secret?"

"Don't think of it as a sickness. Think of it as a gift from God, a gift that must be kept secret for many reasons. Right now, Tony, I want to put your mind at ease."

He paced up and down. "All doctors and specialists have concurred. Now listen carefully. There are unusual tiny chemicals in you that bind together and become very strong. When these tiny chemicals try to get out of your body, they make you feel very uncomfortable. That is when you have to stop whatever it is you are doing, whether it is working, eating, or having sex, and try to relieve yourself. If you can't release anything, this composite continues to build up inside you, but eventually, these chemicals must be released.

Now hold on to your seats!" Milton stopped pacing the floor and spoke with quiet certainty.

"This substance you create inside you has never, ever been found within a living creature before! It is very, very valuable!"

"You're playing with our minds." I said.

"No Tony. Your body's system is creating this. There is something in your secretion glands that manufactures these valuable particles."

"You mean something valuable my son-in-law has?"

"Milton, are you telling me that I can produce something extremely valuable if I just live in my usual abnormal way?" "No. It only becomes valuable if it is processed. You have probably been producing this for years, but it's worthless in its natural state."

Milton came closer to me. "I don't want to tell you too much because--."

"Because I really am dying in a very strange way and you don't want me to know."

"Tony, what can I do to make you believe me? I wish I could get what you have. What a wonderful, wonderful ability you have been blessed with."

Milton put his hands together, looked out my window, raised his eyes to the sky as if praying and said, "I would thank God every day if He gave me your ability. Yes, I would thank you, God. Thank you, God. Thank you, God." Milton looked as if he was having a religious orgasm.

Vera ran over to her son and cradled him in her arms. "I want you should rest. People crazy can make you."

"I am not crazy, Mother! Stop treating me like I am crazy! I know what I am saying."

"Maybe it's from the smells. Maybe crazy you get from the smells. Like your father with onions. From genes, always genes it's from."

"You're not telling us the truth, Milton! I think what you're really saying is that I'm losing my Tony."

Sandra cried as she came over and held me. "We're only married five years, and I won't even have a child to remember him by."

I held her tight, afraid of what I might hear next.

"No! No! No! Listen to me, both of you."

"Also, I maybe should listen too?"

"Tony, you are perfectly well, except for this problem, and you've had it for years and haven't died. But now, you can be made physically comfortable, and at the same time, become wealthy beyond your wildest dreams!"

Milton came over to me and put his hand on my shoulder. "Also, I must tell you, as a doctor and as your brother-in-law, both sides of the situation."

Now he was going to reveal the truth. My head started banging.

Sandra looked up, tears streaming down her face. "Is it cancer, Milton?"

"How long do I have? Tell us!" I insisted.

"It's nothing like that. What you have is a God-given gift!

It's nothing bad. It's about having a choice."

"What kind of a choice?" I asked.

"Your choice is whether you want to keep this gift or safely put a stop to it. There, I told you!"

I couldn't believe what Milton said so I asked him to explain.

"An operation can be done on you that won't be dangerous, but it will permanently stop you from producing this very valuable substance. It can be done in a day. The next day you can go home to live the way you lived before, in your attic apartment, upstairs from my mother."

"Will Tony be well?" Sandra asked smiling as she wiped the tears from her face.

"He won't be bothered by this problem anymore."

"Will we be able to have children?"

"He will be able to have sex which could produce children."

"Could I hold down a job?"

"Nothing would physically stop you. You would function like anyone normally functions. But remember, this operation is not reversible. Once you stop this process in your body, you can never, ever again, produce this substance worth billions and billions of dollars."

"You had no right to keep this from us, Milton! What kind of brother are you? I was sick with worry." Sandra said angrily.

"I guess I should have given you this option earlier."

"You should have told us as soon as you found out, Milton! You and the other doctors had no right to keep it a secret from me. I could sue the doctors and this hospital!"

"My son, a job wouldn't have! Tony, in mine Godfather movies nobody sues!"

"I'm sorry. I am truly sorry. I was only thinking of the fabulous future you two could have."

"Hell of a brother-in-law you turned out to be!"

"There is no choice for us. Tony wants what I want. How soon can he have this operation, Milton?"

"I can schedule it for the day after tomorrow."

Sandra gave me a big kiss and hug.

"Thank God! See, Tony, all those candles I light worked for us." She smiled happily.

I didn't want to upset Sandra, but as Milton's words about the value of what I produced burned into my brain, I suddenly realized I had to know the rest of the story.

"Milton, are there many people who would pay for what I produce?"

"Why do you care about that?" Sandra exploded.

"People throughout the world would pay for what you have."

Sandra looked at us with daggers. "I don't want to hear another thing about this, Milton. Just make plans for that operation as quickly as possible."

I suggested Sandra go home with her mother but she insisted she was going to stay with me until the operation was over.

"I have to tell you, Tony that while many people, companies, institutions, and governments would pay all this money for what you have, others would look for devious methods to get it. That's why I tried to keep it a secret. As soon as we suspected you were producing this substance, the United States government had plainclothes men guard your room."

Vera ran to the door and peeked out. "In plain clothes, he is."

She closed the door. "It's like a movie. Here we got a movie, a real live movie!"

"This is not a movie, Ma!" Sandra said. "This is our life! Tony's in danger. That's why there's a guard! When that reporter puts this story in the newspaper, all the television stations will get it. What will we do then?"

"The Secret Service is going to kill the story." Milton informed us.

"I can't believe the government is in on this. I must be important."

"You can be important throughout the world, Tony. What you have is beneficial to all governments, but our country would want to benefit from it, after all, you are a United States citizen."

"Why did this happen to us?" Sandra moaned.

"Is there any answer, Milton?"

"Only a doctor he is, but I'm telling you it's from mine chicken soup, mine penicillin chicken soup."

"No Mother." Milton explained. "Tony has had this for years. He had it before he met Sandra. He had it before your chicken soup with the gumballs and the snowballs."

"Oy Vey (Dear me), almost another Paul Newman Company I was, now, Horowitz Magic Zoop, down my drain it goes."

I kept thinking about my pending operation. Is this ability of mine a curse or a blessing? Did I really want a normal, mundane existence? How rich and important could I become? Could I throw away what probably is my once in a lifetime opportunity to really be somebody of importance? After years of failure, could I throw away success? But what is success anyway? I think Sandra's idea of success is very different from mine, at least in this situation. Is it because she's a woman?

Is success a sex thing? I've never had sex and only know what an orgasm is from the books I've read and the guys who talk about how they made it with this girl or that girl. Sex sounds unbelievable and I know Sandra wants me to have an orgasm. That's what she prays for when she lights those candles and dresses up in those see-through nightgowns.

Sandra always has orgasms. I read a lot of books on how to get girls to have orgasms without using my penis. Sandra makes a lot of noise when she has one. That's when her mother bangs on the wall. Some of the girls I dated never made noise. I wonder what I would do if I had an orgasm? What if I never had one? Does one miss what one never has?

Sandra and I talked about the guys she dated before we met. She told me everything. I didn't want to hear it, but she said she wanted to start with a clean slate. I told her to wait for Yom Kippur, (holiday of forgiveness) but she couldn't let it go. That day I became Father Costello, my Jewish wife's confessor.

She told me she thought she was in love with one guy, Joey, so they did it. Then she dated some guy named

Bobby for a long time. They did it too. She started to go into detail about how they did it, maybe she thought it would help me function sexually, but it only upset me.

After a while, I told Sandra I didn't want to hear anything about her orgasms with other guys because I didn't like the idea that anyone even kissed her before I did!

Now my whole life has changed. I have an opportunity I never thought I would have. I can't believe what has happened!

If I have this operation, I would be able to get an erection, put my penis inside Sandra, and have an orgasm. I would be a real man like I was meant to be, and that's what Sandra wants.

I could get a job, but I couldn't become a banker or a lawyer because this thing I have, ruined my school years.

Sandra would continue to work and have kids, which Vera would bring up and feed them lots of onions. We would be middle-class American citizens, just what my wife always wanted us to be.

Sandra's voice stopped my thoughts.

"All right, Milton, let's get back to the original question. Why did this happen to Tony?"

"We are not sure. The only answer I can give you is that it could be caused by Tony's genes. It's too bad his parents are not alive so we could check them out, but obviously, they had no problem having sex.

Often when a person has a disability, new abilities appear, or other abilities become stronger. For instance, some people who are blind have exceptional hearing power. People can't speak sometimes can hear, see, think or memorize extremely well. Others can do mathematical problems faster than a calculator. John Nash suffered from the mental disability of schizophrenia, but another part of his mind was exceptional and he won the Nobel Prize.

Sometimes the body compensates and this seems to be what has happened to Tony's body. His gift can be a great thing or a terrible burden. It can be whatever you choose to make of it.

We have always looked for answers to why some people are gifted, most of the time, scientific studies point to the genes." "Well, I've made my choice." Sandra said.

"Do you agree with Sandra, Tony?"

"I need time to think about it."

I looked up as Sandra leaned over my bed, looked me in the face, and said in a very, very serious tone.

"There is nothing to think about! You can't stay this way! Now's your chance to be a real husband, to be like other men, to enjoy the things that other normal men enjoy with their wives." I didn't say anything.

"If there is no alternative operation, I will stick by you, Tony, but now you have to make a decision, either the operation or it's over between us."

We looked deeply into each other's eyes.

"You mean you would leave me if I decide against the reversal operation?" Sandra avoided looking at me, but I saw the tears cascading down her cheeks as she went out the door.

Sandra didn't come to see me and wouldn't talk to me on the phone, but Vera visited me every day.

"My daughter, thinking she is not. All the time, I talk to her, and always she cries, then to the door she shows me. What I can do, I don't know.

Milton, every day he comes and talks to her and him she shows the door. What to do, we don't know.

Only like a big watermelon she wants you should make her. Only a child to love she wants. But love for you Tony, she has."

"So why won't she listen to how I feel about the operation? I haven't even made a decision yet."

"Me, I don't tell anybody what to do, but how I feel Tony, you know."

"Sure, I know, Ma."

"My daughter, like her mother she's not. My daughter, she is different."

"I wouldn't want her any other way, Ma."

"A little crazy, a little mixed up she is."

"Why else would she marry me, Ma?"

"That, I didn't say. That, you said. About who she marries, I could talk, but I won't."

"We've been there, Ma. Let's not go there again."

"But such opportunity now she has! Smart with her, you must be, Tony."

"She won't even talk to me. It's been a week!"

I felt down, and nothing my mother-in-law said made me feel any better. I didn't know what to do. Eventually, Vera gave up and left.

A little later, Milton came in.

"Don't let my sister get to you! Remember, like Superman, you are a man with more than human powers. You must forgo fleeting, transient pleasures for something much bigger!"

"Easy for you to say, Milton. You're out there fucking at the drop of whatever."

"It's not that great, believe me. I'd rather be you! You have the opportunity to be remembered like Edison, Madam Curie, and Leonardo de Vinci. You can be a Robin Hood to the world! Any idiot can have sex!"

Milton left and I turned over and dreamed of being an idiot who was having sex.

The next day Vera came in with Milton, carrying a large box.

"I gave special permission to Mama to bring you dinner."

This was the only thing that would give me temporary consolation. Mama's brisket and even her string beans tasted fantastic because she knew the secret of how to disguise the poison of our world, sugar, with onions.

"Like a bomb, it doesn't kill. Only a little longer it takes." She said.

"I don't care about living." I said as I ate Vera's delicious meal. "My life is a mess. The one woman in the world I love has left me without even hearing me out!"

"Tony, Tony." Vera whispered in my ear.

I looked up from my food and saw Sandra standing in the doorway.

"I couldn't stay away."

She came over to my bed and kissed me on my lips. "I love you, Tony."

She sat down on my bed.

"Sometimes I'm stubborn, like a mule. I should learn to listen. I made a mistake by walking out. I'm sorry."

Milton stood up and applauded.

"Now, that's a baby sister I can be proud of!"

"Do you want, maybe we should leave?" Vera asked.

"No. Stay here. We have to talk because I need answers to questions, Milton." Sandra said.

"I don't know what I would have done if you didn't come back, Sandra. I'm glad you didn't give up on me."

"We've gone through too much together to throw it all away, Tony. I'm willing to listen. But how long is it safe to wait to have this operation?"

"Sandra, Tony can have this reversal operation at any time in the future."

"Are you sure, Milton? Are you positive?"

"We can do it whenever you decide you want it. That's a guarantee from all the doctors and specialists. You don't have to worry about that.

If you decide not to have the operation now, Tony, we will continue care outside the hospital and make you as physically comfortable as possible. I, my colleagues, and the scientists will monitor you after you leave here, and will routinely check you at your home and this hospital.

Each day we will collect what you have done because it can't be left around in its original state. We can't waste something that can become so valuable. Then it will be processed, evaluated, and stored away in a secret place by our government.

Once a month, you will receive a statement of its worth, and you will be able to buy anything you want."

There was a deafening silence, and once again, we all looked at each other.

"I want to see it! I want to see what it looks like after it's processed." I said.

Milton put in a phone call to have a sample of it brought in.

Vera was thrilled. "So excited I am. Such a special event."

"Better than having a grandchild, Ma?"

Sandra had hit the nail on the head. That's exactly how I felt. It's like I gave birth to a baby and was about to see it for the first time. I couldn't wait. My very own million-dollar baby that I carried for forty years!

A half-hour went by. Three-quarters of an hour passed. What happened to my baby?

A few minutes later, an armed guard opened my door. Another guard entered with a small black metal box. Milton took the black box from the guard and asked him to wait outside.

He carried the box over to my bed as Sandra and Vera looked on. He opened the black metal box and took out a small glass case, and we all looked inside.

There it was! This is what all the fuss is about, a small, shiny, smooth, round, dark gold object, about the size of a dime.

"What you are looking at has been purified and polished. The metallurgist worked on this as specialists work on diamonds." Milton said.

Vera couldn't take her eyes off it. "From nothing, my Milton, he makes money. A genius he is!"

Vera kissed Milton on his head while Sandra cringed at her mother's attitude.

I didn't care who got the credit. I laughed. I howled. I jumped on the bed.

"Bell, bell (beautiful, beautiful). My prodotto (product) is stupendo (marvelous)!"

I danced around the room while everyone tried to calm me and get me into bed. My private nurse came running into the room, and Milton had her give me a pill. I lay down, and Sandra sat and washed my face with a wet towel.

How was I expected to act? Milton just compared my little creation to a diamond.

"What do you think this one little creation of mine is worth, Milton?"

"I don't want to get excited again, tony. I'll tell you another day."

"No! I want to know now! I have a right to know!"

Milton looked in the box. "This little piece is worth over twenty thousand dollars."

"Twenty thousand?" Sandra asked.

"Twenty thousand?" Vera questioned.

I tried to figure out how much I would be worth if I made a delivery every day.

As the guards took the little box away, Milton continued talking.

"You should know that what was in that box and everything you have produced since you came into this hospital belongs to you. We, I mean, the hospital, have no right to it. Just like when a dentist takes out old gold fillings from a patient's teeth, the gold still belongs to the patient.

If, of course, you care to contribute any of this to the hospital or to science for

further studies, that would be greatly appreciated. We could even add another building to the hospital in your name.

"Are you positively sure Tony can have an operation later, Milton?" Sandra asked again.

"No problem. Just remember, once Tony's power is taken away, he will never, ever again, be able to get it back."

"I know. I know that. But I can't help thinking that I could have a baby if Tony had the operation. Mama, wouldn't it be wonderful to have a grandchild?"

"When empty is the stomach, so is the brain! Go eat something." Vera replied.

Milton spoke more of the operation. He said he wanted us to understand everything before we made our decision.

"This operation would alleviate the area where your intestinal mixtures meet your fluids and jell together to become hard and valuable. This substance, which gives you your ability, will then be channeled to leave your body normally without meeting your other fluids. There is a lot to think about before you and Sandra make up your mind. You have three options.

Tony, you are capable of becoming the wealthiest, most famous, and powerful man in the world. You would be able to fill the bellies of the poor in all countries, all over the world.

Your option is to have this operation and permanently reverse this ability you now have.

Your last option is to stay the way you are for a time, see how you enjoy living as a famous billionaire, and have this operation at any time you choose in the future."

I was still in shock about what was happening.

"Don't decide anything now. "Milton advised as he put his arms around us. "Make the most of this magical feeling. Be happy. You and Sandra have a unique life to look forward to if you decide to keep this power. If you decide against it, well, that's your choice." He kissed Sandra and Vera and left.

Vera came over to us, took our hands in hers, and said, "If onions on your brains didn't grow, what you should do, you know." Then he kissed us both and went out the door.

Sandra curled up next to me on the bed.

"I still don't want to accept what has happened to us, Tony."

"I know Sandra, but how can we throw all this away? I never had anything as a child.

I was never given anything in my whole life. Even my parents were taken away from me. Now I've been this gift. It is my chance to help so many, many people like myself who have nothing. Wouldn't it be sacrilegious to destroy this gift I've been given?"

"Hold me, Tony. I've missed you. My bed is cold at home without you."

I kissed her, and we fell asleep together. When Sandra woke me, it was dusk.

"I'm going home, Tony. I want you to think quietly by yourself. It is really your decision to make. If I tell you to get this operation and something happens to you, I would not be able to live with myself. I'll be here tomorrow. I love you."

We kissed again and again, and then she left me all alone to wonder and decide about my advantageous but very strange situation.

V

It is after seven o'clock in the evening and getting dark. I've finished dinner, and Betty, my private nurse, has sponged me and given me a rub down to help me relax, but my thoughts won't let me sleep.

Am I being fair to Sandra? Am I thinking only of wealth and fame? Would Sandra adjust to this other lifestyle, or would it put even more stress on our marriage?

How upsetting would that be not to have children? What kind of world would we bring our kids into anyway? Besides, women are having children later in life, and Sandra's only forty. Maybe we could adopt children from starving countries and give them the best of everything. In fact, with this great wealth, I could feed and clothe hundreds and hundreds of needy children wherever they are.

I would be able to aid people who are out of work and help fight terrorism. I could give money to people who lost all their savings in the stock market. I would help fight aids, cancer, and other sicknesses. There is no end to what I would do!

The more I thought, the more I realized I must be crazy to even entertain thoughts of having an operation that would stop me from doing all this!

Besides, if I stay the way I am, I will be made comfortable by excellent doctors and have the finest of everything.

But, best of all, I would not have to live in my Mother-in-law's house! Yippee! That thought helped convince me to forget about the operation.

Suddenly, my door was opened, and a hospital gurney was wheeled into my room by a big two-hundred-pound nurse I've never seen before.

She closed the door, told me she was taking over for my private nurse and that her name was Evelyn. She pulled out a long hypodermic needle from her bag and told me to roll over on my stomach.

"What's that for? Where's my regular nurse? She always says goodnight to me before she leaves and brings in the other private nurse. What's going on?"

"Some changes were made. I've special orders for the lab." She turned me over, held me down, and jabbed me with the needle.

"The lab is closed. It's never open after seven." I said.

She pressed my face into the pillow but from the corner of my eye, I saw she was ready with another needle. I quickly raised my army and knocked it from her hand.

"You bastard!" she yelled in my ear.

I tried to fight the weak feeling that came over me but the shot was beginning to work. She turned me over and I started to yell, but she buried my face in her huge breasts.

I turned my head sideways. "You're a crazy nurse! What do you want?"

She didn't answer. Her saucer-like eyes just stared at me. Then she whispered in my ears. "I'm taking you into the laundry room so no one will disturb us."

The needle had taken full effect and I had no strength to fight her off. I was a toy in her hands. She pulled me on top of the gurney.

"They will be looking for me. My wife and the doctors will be looking for me." I said in a weak voice.

As we left my room I hoped to see the guard who always stood outside my door, but he was gone. She wheeled me down the hall as I murmured. "Take me back or you'll get fired."

"I'm not worried.' She answered. As we came to the laundry room she looked around, then quickly pushed me inside and locked the door

"I picked a perfect time for this. The staffs are busy eating so no one will miss you and no one will disturb us." She said as she gave a hearty laugh, raised my hospital gown, and stared at my body.

I grabbed the sides of the gurney and tried to lift myself up as she pushed me down and tied my hands to the rails.

"You're too weak to move, so just leave everything to me. I'll do the work for both of us."

She put her lips against mine, and I was unable to push her away. I felt the room spin as this crazy Amazon nurse climbed on top of me.

"Why are you doing this?" I cried.

She didn't answer, just smiled as she pulled her clothes off and let her huge ding-a-lings dance on my face.

"Just be my friend for a few minutes, then, I'll let you go."

She dropped her two-hundred pounds on my body. "Ugh," I moaned as my bones cracked and my stomach sank. She grabbed my penis. "What a little thing!" She cried out in disappointment. "I expected a Big Mac. You're only a little sausage."

"Get off me!" My voice cracked. I couldn't breathe. I tried to kick the bitch off but to no avail. I started to regurgitate as her two-hundred pounds went up and down on my body.

A sudden banging on the door filled me with hope, but she quickly covered my mouth with her hands.

"We're busy in here," she yelled.

I bit her hand. She quickly pushed my jaws shut.

"I have to drop off some things." The voice on the other side of the door called out.

"Leave them there. I'll take them in when we're finished in here."

"Okay." The voice replied.

I felt a cold sweat come over my body as I heard steps walk away down the corridor. I was a prisoner.

"Don't worry, little man, I'm not going to hurt you. I heard what that newspaper reporter said when he was here. That's when I decided I wanted a child by you. There is a strong possibility your child will inherit your ability. I read all your reports, so I know all about you."

She took her hands from my mouth.

"What are you talking about? If you read my reports, you know I can't get anyone pregnant! That's part of my problem!"

"I'm not buying that story! We are going to have sex. We can start any way you want, but it has to end with intercourse because it's my time of the month to conceive."

"Any sexual feeling I get causes an upset stomach, then I lose my sexual ability. You're a nurse. You have to believe my reports!"

"Who says I'm a nurse? I'm here because of you. I'm here to become the mother of your child!"

"Believe me. I can't get you pregnant! My body doesn't work right, that's why I'm here. Right now, my stomach is acting up. I need to get to a bathroom!"

"Just relax. You don't need a bathroom. You need a good lay!"

She tried and tried to get me inside her.

"What's with you? You need more incentive?"

"I told you I'm not able to have sex, so I can't get you pregnant!

My wife has tried everything possible for years and years she's tried."

"Hang on." She cried. "I'll get you bigger. I'll get you up there if I have to use a splint! Now, invade me, invade me!" She demanded.

She tried to ride me then looked down at my little limp, long-suffering organ. "You're not excited. I'll get you excited."

With that remark, she started to lick my face and kept going down my body. It reminded me of Vera's funny onion story, but this was nothing to laugh about. I was in pain, sweating from nerves, and sick to my stomach.

I began to wonder if my body's ability changed since I came to the hospital. My problems were not as often as when I first came in. What if, by some strange quirk of fate, I get this crazy pregnant? What if she tells Sandra? What if she proves it in court and demands money? What if? What if? What if? This is all a nightmare! No, I opened my eyes. This is not a nightmare! It's really happening.

"My fire is burning hot so get it straight and strong and fertilize me, boy! Don't make me resort to other methods." She said as she nuzzled her tongue inside my ear.

I closed my eyes, hoping she would disappear, and concentrated on my stomach pains. Again she hoisted herself on top of me. "Maybe you want me to tie you up and whip you. Would that turn you on?"

"I need a cigarette." I said. "I need it bad."

"You don't smoke. I read it in your chart."

'I need the toilet for you until I get what I want!" she announced.

I closed my eyes and prayed this punishment would stop. I promised the Almighty I would never treat my Mother-in-law badly again. I promised I would love her and treat her with the utmost respect if He would only free me from this inhuman creature.

As I brushed a sweaty face against the pillow, I suddenly heard voices in the corridor. I started to yell, but she covered my mouth and grabbed my penis. I cringed with pain!

She held up a knife. "Once more, you try to yell, and I'll cut it off." She stuffed my mouth with a towel until the voices drifted down the corridor, then pulled the towel from my mouth and covered my tongue with hers. I could taste the garlic from her last meal.

I prayed for help. God, somebody help me. When is someone going to look for me? Why doesn't Sandra phone and ask where I am? Isn't the guard back from his dinner break? What about the doctors, the nurses, my mother-in-law? My prayers were pointless. No one would find me alive under this massive body of flesh!

I thought of Sandra and how she lit the candles and how we tried to make love. The thought of Sandra comforted me while I suffered from evil Evelyn, who bounced up and down, up and down on my body.

Then, what was that? Was someone moving the door handle?

"Hey, we need to get into this room. Who's in here? Answer me and open up or I'll help and break open the door!"

Evil Evelyn went to the door and listened until she heard footsteps walk away.

"I've got to get out of here!" she moaned.

She gagged me with the towel and tied my feet together with hospital tape. Quickly she pulled on her uniform, peeked out the door, and blew me a kiss.

"Goodbye, Italian stallion. You are a big disappointment." As soon as she left, I pushed the towel out of my mouth with my tongue and hollered, but no one answered.

My hands were still taped to the side rails of the gurney but I managed to raise myself up and gradually rip off the tape with the teeth. Then, with my sore hands, tore the tape from my ankles and fell to the floor.

I flew down the hall, my naked backside exposed by my open hospital gown that flapped like a pair of blue wings on a bird. I was free!

A nurse approached me. "You poor thing, you must be from the psychiatric section. I'll bring you to the other side of the hospital. They must be looking for you."

I tried to tell her what happened as I walked with her, but she was sure I was hallucinating. I stamped my feet and shook my head.

"No! I don't come from the psychiatric ward! Listen to me!"

"Calm down. I don't want to call for help! We are almost there."

As we walked down the hall, a nurse recognized me.

"Tony Costello! We've looked all over for you!"

When she told the other nurse who I was, she apologized to me, and they quickly put me in a wheelchair and rushed me to my room.

Milton was nervously waiting with other doctors and guards. "I was raped! Raped! Do you hear me? Right here in your hospital! What kind of a place is this?"

I yelled. I shouted. I didn't care who heard me. I wanted everyone to know what happened!

Milton tried to give me pills to calm me, but I threw them on the floor.

"It isn't safe here! Give me my clothes. I'm going home!"

I ran around looking for my clothes, but they were gone. "You need to relax and get over this, Tony. You wouldn't want Sandra to see you like this."

"I don't want Sandra to know! No one must tell Sandra or Vera! I don't want them to know anything about this, or I'll never hear the end of it!"

The police who guarded the hospital came in, and I told them what happened and described my attacker. They surrounded the hospital and searched everywhere for hours, but evil Evelyn was gone.

My private nurse, Betty, was found tied and gagged in a closet but was not hurt. She was very frightened and was taken home.

Double guards were put outside my door, and Milton gave me an injection so I would sleep. Eventually, my head stopped pounding, and my stomach stopped hurting. As I drifted off to sleep, I murmured to my brother-in-law, "No more nurses. No operations. I am going home."

I was wide awake at dawn and anxious to leave, but Milton came in with two CIA men who wanted all the details about last night.

Jack Spears and Dave Lang took notes on the whole gory story and then had the nerve to ask me if the woman was a friend of mine from the past.

I was angry as hell! I was boiling over! Imagine, after what I went through, they thought it was an inside job! I told them where to go in no uncertain Italian.

"Calm down, calm down, Mr. Costello, we have to cover all aspects of the case, so don't be upset by the questions we are required to ask."

"Just how often do rapes happen in hospitals?" I was curious.

They told me it was very rare and only happened to me because a deranged woman discovered my unusual circumstances.

After they left, I was allowed to shower, shave and get dressed by myself. It felt good to walk around. As Nurse Betty and I waited for a wheelchair to bring me downstairs, I turned on my television and couldn't believe what I saw.

Milton came in.

"Look." I pointed to the TV. "I thought the government was going to kill the story."

"I know. I know. This wasn't supposed to happen! I'm sorry, Tony."

I turned the channels.

"I'm on all the TV stations, even the religious one! Listen to what they say about me."

"We believe heaven has sent us this God-like creature. He, like Jesus, is the miracle of our century. This heavenly being has come to us in our hour of need."

"Are they crazy, comparing me to Jesus?"

Milton turned down the volume as Sandra rushed in. "Tony, you're on the TV and in the newspapers! This is dangerous. What's going to happen?"

Vera walked in and happily announced.

"Famous we are. On televisions, everyone watches mine picture, mine son, mine daughter, and even mine son-in-law."

Vera went over to Milton and kissed him.

"This was not supposed to be made public, Mother."

"So, it's so bad? Should I mind being famous?"

"But Tony's safety is now in jeopardy!" Sandra screamed.

The telephone rang, and Vera answered.

"Grand Central Station, how can I help you?" Vera listened. "He says from Hollywood, he is. Buddy Butler, he calls himself. Butlers, I'll tell him we don't need it yet. Hello—"

Milton took the phone and yelled.

"Just who are you calling?

We don't need an agent. This is not a theatrical show!" He banged the receiver.

Again the phone rang. Milton angrily answered.

"Hello! This is Dr. Horowitz!" Milton was silent for a long time.

"Yes, Sir." He listened attentively.

"We would be honored." He continued to listen.

"Whatever time you say. We will wait for your call. Thank you, Sir."

Milton hung up, obviously shaken.

"That was the President of the United States."

"He called me? He called himself? Why didn't you let me speak?" I yelled.

"He wants to meet you at the White House. His secretary will call and make an appointment."

Sandra squealed. "We are going to the White House."

"Oh, such an honor! What to wear, I don't know," Vera cried.

Just then, two men came in and asked for Dr. Milton Horowitz. They showed Milton.

MAKING IT: MEDICAL COMEDY IN BROOKLYN

their identification and we were introduced to Detective Reardon and Detective Robert McPherson from the Secret Service. Milton told us to listen and do everything they said.

They explained how Sandra and I would be secretly escorted out of the hospital while Vera would deter the media from following us.

"How? How do I deter? She asked.

The detectives instructed Vera to go downstairs where, the TV cameras and newspaper reporters were waiting for news about me. They told her to be sure to say we already left the hospital.

Thrilled to be of such importance, Vera quickly went to the mirror, fixed herself up, threw a kiss to her reflection, then to us, and excitedly ran to the cameras.

While we all watched, Vera made her television debut on Good Morning America.

"Tell us, Mrs. Horowitz, how does it feel being the Mother-in-law of such a famous young man?"

"Oh, so happy I feel. My family, already they are home many hours. Away with the taxi they went."

"I guess we will have to interview them at another time."

"Never fear, the whole story I will tell, so everyone should know." Vera took a deep breath. "Milton son, Milton S. Horowitz, all this he discovered. You should know he was the finder. Milton, my son the proc-tol-o-gist, with golden fingers, was born.

My daughter, her heart is from gold.

Mine son-in-law, such a son-in-law! From the sky, the golden sun shined on his belly and boom-boom, plop-plop here it was, the miracle."

I started to shut off the TV so we could go downstairs to the ambulance, and make our getaway, when we noticed a man on television, pushed himself through the crowd to Vera.

"I'm Ed Rooney, and you should know your son-in-law needs an agent. I'm that agent! Here's my card. I'm talking movies, nightclubs. I'm talking total representation. But if he won't do it we'll pay you ten thousand dollars if you'll appear one night in a nightclub."

We couldn't wait to see if Vera accepted because the Secret Service men put Sandra and I on stretchers covered our faces with empty oxygen masks and carried us to the ambulance that was waiting to take us to a secluded house on Long Island. They said they would follow in unmarked cars and warned us in case of trouble, we should be prepared for a wild trip.

Sandra's eyes were filled with fear as they took us downstairs and into the ambulance. Then at high speed, we left the hospital grounds.

Sandra's hand clutched mine. We were on our way. I didn't know what lay ahead, but I did know I wouldn't need to take the D train to the Bronx anymore. I was in big business now. It was a dangerous business, but my very own, very lucrative business.

I wondered if I should try to look more like a businessman. Maybe I should get an attaché case and a Chesterfield top-coat. Maybe we should move to some ritzy section of New York, and get luxury cars and join the country club. I tried to talk to Sandra about this, but she was too nervous to listen.

I was nervous too, but I couldn't stop thinking how lucky I was. I may not be a Yalee, but right now, little Mr. Nobody was a celebrity!

It seemed like hours before the ambulance slowed down. It was another half hour before we stopped. The guards who rode with us took off our oxygen masks and blankets, and I put my arm around Sandra and rubbed her back.

"How do you feel?"

Before she had a chance to answer, the ambulance started to move again. I looked out the window and saw massive, black, iron gates opening to let us pass. Two guards stood at the gates and watched us as we went through. We proceeded up a hill to an extraordinarily huge and beautiful stone house, where we stopped and were helped out of the ambulance. We walked up the stairs to the large front double door entrance, where a serious-looking, older, black man greeted us. He said his name was Hiram Jones and that we should not worry because we are safe here. The Secret Service men knew Hiram and informed us that in his younger days, he had worked for the FBI, and would take good care of us.

Guards entered the house with us and spoke to Hiram about details concerning our stay. Hiram said he had been informed and taken care of everything. Our guards left the room, but Hiram told us they would remain in the house indefinitely to ensure our safety.

As Sandra and I walked around the living room admiring the dark, elegant architecture and furnishing a jovial-looking, rotund lady wearing a white apron came in.

"Greetings, greetings, I am Amelia, the cook, and I do magic in the kitchen. Whatever I can make for you will be my pleasure. I have worked in this house for twenty-five years. The government originally owned it, then Dr. Tong and his family bought it, but it is up for sale again, and I am very sad because it is my home, and I wouldn't want to move."

Amelia and Hiram made us feel very comfortable, but Hiram warned us never to go off the property by ourselves. He said he or a guard would drive us wherever we needed to go.

"I don't understand. I thought I would have my own car to drive around or to go to my office." I said.

"Oh no, Mr. Tony, we must guard you so no one takes advantage of you. You must have your office right here in this house."

Sandra and I were very disappointed.

"Tony, it sounds like we are virtually prisoners in this palace."

"I'm sure it's only going to be this way temporarily. Things will change, you'll see."

Sandra and I went and explored the house. We discovered there were eighteen huge rooms, ten elegant bathrooms, and six garages with four expensive cars. I felt like a king, and I hadn't seen my whole castle.

A few days later, the Secret Service managed to have our clothes and personal things brought to us from our apartment in Vera's house. Due to secrecy, Vera was not told where we lived or our private phone number, and she was not allowed to visit us. Sandra and her mother were very angry about this, but I couldn't do anything about it, not that I tried.

I was very busy because I was on schedule carefully planned by my doctors. Milton had a nurse visit me every day to keep my body in working order and to arrange for my deposits. She consulted with Amelia about my special diet and my exercise schedule.

I discovered there was a gym in this huge house every day out with a private trainer. I even had my very own pool! I felt stupendo (marvelous)! What a life!

Tons of mail started arriving here from our old address, but before we received it a government clearing center checked it, and then our private secretary went over it.

Strangers wrote to me and blessed me, others begged for money. Girls sent nude photos and offered me their bodies. Many wrote they loved me and proposed marriage.

Sandra had a hard time handling this mail, so she tore them up every day. I missed those ego-building letters.

It took hours to go over the offers for me to advertise products from food companies, medical companies, and toilet paper companies. Restaurants and hotels wanted to pay me to go there. Movies made me unbelievable offers, and people and relatives I never heard of wrote and invited me to use their facilities, thinking they could benefit from my internal disorder.

Colleges and universities offered me honorary degrees just to visit. Hospitals asked for contributions, and I gladly sent checks to all worthwhile institutions.

Milton said I should not have yelled at the President of the New York Stock exchange for offering me my own special seat in my own special room away from all the other stockholders. Sometimes I resented being used!

There was no shortage of invitations, and if it wasn't dangerous for me, Sandra and I could have traveled the world as guests. We were invited to visit every country and become citizens because everyone wanted a piece of the action.

The latest thing was a cartoon movie of me as the Green Dollar Dragon who traveled the world and dropped money wherever he went.

The Lifestyles of the Rich and Famous wanted to televise how we lived.

Write-ups about me were constantly in the newspapers and I had dozens of book and magazine offers.

Vera was hassled constantly by reporters who wanted to know our address, which the CIA still didn't allow her to have her own safety.

The Secret Service kept an eye on Vera, expecting the possibility of her being kidnapped and the demand for a large ransom. Meanwhile, Milton said she loved all the attention but kept asking him for our address.

Eventually, our unlisted phone number was discovered by strangers who threatened us, unless we sent them money. We had to change our number again and again.

The newscasters started referring to me as, The Dynamo money Machine. This really upset me! I was no machine. I had a soul! I was flesh and blood! Someone loved me, and I loved back. I was a human being!

One night, as Sandra and I watched TV, we saw a march in Times Square. People held signs that read, 'WE WANT TONY ON THE BALLOT', 'VOTE FOR TONY, HE MAKES MONEY FOR MEDICARE,' and 'TONY CAN SAVE SOCIAL SECURITY!'

It was all true. I was doing these things. I cannot believe the money my accountants and lawyers told me I made. They say I can live like a king, and I do. I'm always on the throne.

47

The next day as I sat doing my work, Hiram Jones knocked on my dear to tell me the president's secretary was on the phone. I quickly dropped my business, pulled up my pants, and picked up the phone.

"Yes sir, this is Anthony Costello." I stood and listened as the president's secretary invited Sandra and I to the White House the following Wednesday. He said we would be picked up at ten A.M. at our home, but I was not to tell anyone about it except Hiram Jones, who could be trusted completely. He said our guards, who were part of the Secret Service, would be notified about our trip at the proper time.

I thanked him, said we were honored by the invitation, and looked forward to the visit.

Sandra was very excited, but I had to argue with her not to call Vera and tell her.

The next Wednesday, at precisely ten AM, we heard a strange noise above our home. Hiram called us to come outside where the guards stood watching a helicopter land on our front lawn.

Two pilots out of the plane introduced themselves and showed Hiram their credentials.

Sandra gave me a fearful look and refused to enter the helicopter. Hiram gradually eased her fears as he explained the safety of the plane and the experience of the pilots. Then he took her arm and helped her into the executive aircraft. I noticed both pilots carried guns, and when they took off, another helicopter followed us. It was a great experience, but Sandra wasn't happy until we landed on the White House lawn.

We were briskly escorted into the executive mansion and to a private room where we were served a wonderful brunch.

As soon as we finished, we were taken into the Oval Office, which was filled with important people like the Vice President, Secretary of the State, the Secretary of the Treasury, Director of the Secret Service, head of the FBI, and others who introduced themselves.

A few minutes later, the President came in, shook our hands, and thanked us for coming. Everyone sat down and listened to him speak as he focused his eyes on me.

"Anthony, our government funds are drained. Since September eleventh, we are in dire need of money to fight terrorism. We need more people in the CIA, FBI, and other intelligence agencies. We need to subsidize the airlines and railroads and keep Social Security alive. This war has cost our country billions of dollars, but with your help, we could survive this fiscal crisis."

Everyone stood up, turned to me, and applauded. The President looked at me and began to speak again.

"We want to give you an important position in our government. We want your input, and we want to use your expertise. Can we count on you?"

The room was very, very quiet. I stood up.

"This is my country, Mr. President. I love my country. I will do anything I can to help. You just have to name it. The only thing that bothers me, Mr. President, is that I don't know anything about government work."

"That is not important, Anthony. I didn't know anything when I started. I learn as I go along. It's a matter of trial, error, and putting smart people in the right places, and you, Anthony, are one of those people. What we need to do is put you in the right position!"

Again everyone stood up, faced me, and applauded,

"Mr. President, I just want to know if I will only be a figurehead, or will I be able to make moves that count?"

"You, Tony, will make the most important moves in the country. The whole world will be noting each of your moves. Both the republicans and Democrats will be behind you. They will back every movement you make!"

The President came over to me. "I now present you with the gold key which will open the doors to the rooms where you will do all your important business for our government."

The President handed me the gold key, and everyone applauded. The head of the CIA stood up and said.

"You are the new weapon that can help us keep our country safe and prosperous. We have a partnership, and this partnership must be protected against other countries and people who will try to take you from us. We will do everything to guard you and your family. We commend you for your bravery!"

Everyone stood up and applauded, but I saw the worried look on Sandra's face.

The Vice President continued.

"You will have your own private office, Anthony, and we are in the process of building an attached area to your office with suitable seating. This is where your deliveries will be profiled, purified, and packed. Is everything satisfactory so far?"

I shook my head in the affirmative.

"An armored Brinks truck will come to your home each day, and the guards will pick up your deposits. You are always welcome to do your work here at the White House, but we especially look forward to meeting with you once a month so we can review your progress."

The President stood up. "Our country is very lucky to have you, and we intend to keep you safe! God bless America, and God bless you!"

"These papers state that the United States Government supersedes all other causes that you will be asked to contribute to. Is this agreeable?"

"Of course," I said as I signed.

We all shook hands and were escorted to the helicopter. Once inside, I put my arm around Sandra.

"Tony, you are a hero. You will be doing great things to help our country."

"We, both of us, will be doing great things for our country. I wouldn't be able to do it without a wife who is willing to stand by her man."

"I want to stand by you, Tony, but will this always be our way of life?"

"Let's take each day as it comes, honey."

I looked out the window. "We're landing. We're home. I could get used to this mode of travel."

"I know you could; that's the trouble!" Sandra answered with a slight pout.

That night, as we undressed for bed, Sandra complained to me about the Secret Service men.

"Before I dress or shower, I have to check our bedroom because yesterday, I found one asleep in my closet and the other day I found one watching TCV in our bed! I know we have to be guarded, but I want to lock our bedroom door!"

"You know we're not allowed to lock them out, Sandra. They have to see that we are safe at all times. That's their job."

"But we don't have any freedom! We are never alone and don't go anywhere unless we have guards. I can't remember the last time we went out together to eat or see a show. I feel like a prisoner! I'm not happy living this way. Are you happy, Tony?"

I stroked her bareback. She looked so desirable in her black lace nightgown.

"I would be the happiest man alive if you were content, Sandra. I have everything, everything I could possibly want. I have a wonderful wife who I love. I am famous and making a fortune! I can't believe what has happened to me! I had nothing, and as your mother put it, I was a nebbish (nothing). Now, look at me. I'm somebody. I have status, position."

"Position! That's the problem. Everything depends on your position, and it's always the same one. A sitting one!"

Sandra paced the floor.

"All that's important to you, Tony, is moneta, moneta, moneta (money)!"

"No, Sandra, you are important to me. I love you. You don't appreciate how lucky we are. You should be walking in clouds."

"Oh, yes, White Cloud, on the company that just sent us five thousand rolls." She moved over to the other side of the bed. "Don't talk to me anymore. I'm going to sleep."

The next day, when I spoke to Milton, I told him how unhappy his sister was. He insisted on calling his friend, Dudley Germaine, a psychologist, who began seeing us three times a week.

Things seemed much better, and Sandra started going into the city to shop and see shows, but she always wore a disguise and had Secret Service men with her.

I really felt Dr. Germaine's therapy was working until one rainy day, a few months later, when I walked into our library and found her crying.

"We have this beautiful home but no children who can enjoy it."

I sat down next to her in front of the fireplace, put my arm around her, and kissed her wet cheek, as a guard tip-toed out of the room.

"Maybe we should talk about adopting, Sandra. We can children everything they need or could want."

"What kind of life would they have, Tony? I would be afraid someone would kidnap them. They wouldn't be able to go out and play without guards. Other parents would be afraid to endanger their own kids by letting them play with ours. Children from plain families are being kidnapped, raped, and killed every day, so what chance would ours have?

Besides, no adoption agency would give us a child. We couldn't even fill out the forms as normal people. Like, for instance, what would you say you do for a living?"

"I'm a manufacturer." She gave me one of her looks.

"Ok, OK, I get your point, but you can't dwell on this. There must be something I can do t get you into a better frame of mind."

"Nothing. There is nothing you can do." She wiped her face. "You want to go out?"

"You mean with our guards?'

"No, just the two of us."

"No guards?'

"No guards. I'll dress up as someone else, just like you do. I'll wear a wig."

"You don't have a wig."

"I'll wear one of yours."

"You would dress up as a woman? Don't make me laugh."

"That's what I'm trying to do, honey. I want you to laugh and be happy." I put my arms around her and kissed her.

"Life has played a trick on us, Sandra, but we love each other, and that's what counts." I kissed her again and held her tight. It was a nice, long kiss, just like the old days. Her tongue slid between my lips and into my mouth, but there were no candles, and her clothes didn't drop to the floor

"Tony, you could have the reversal operation. That would make me very, very happy."

"I know. I know. But how can we go backward? Even if the two of us worked, we couldn't make the money I'm making now."

"But honey, millions of people live like that. It's normal. You wouldn't have this horrible sickness, the Midas touch. Who needs it? Besides, I want my own baby!"

"Sandra, you know all about the money we get from my product. Well, I'm putting a lot of it away for our future."

"You're selling our souls to the devil!" There was a long silence.

"Do you think we will die this way, Tony?'

"No, because as I get older I may not be able to keep my business going. This week I produced less than last week." "Are you upset, Tony?"

"There's nothing I can do about it. I'll wait and see what happens. It probably wouldn't be so bad living like normal people. I would be able to do something I wanted to do for so long, long time."

Sandra smiled. "What have you wanted to do for a long, long time, Tony?"

"I want to do what other people do, normal people do. Something I've looked forward to for years."

I held Sandra close and looked into her eyes.

"Say it, Tony. Tell me. What it is that you've waited for and want to do. Put it into words. I need you to talk to me, Tony. Tell me how you want this as much as I do."

Sandra held me tighter.

"Sandra, I'm going to tell you what I want and how I want to do it. It's really important to me. It's hard living this way knowing I can't do it."

"I know, baby. It's difficult for me too." Sandra kissed me and held me tight.

"I want it so bad, honey. It will be so great to finally do it if I ever become normal. Yes, I want this with all my might. I will be the happiest man alive when I can do it!"

"Say it! Say it, Tony! Say you want it as much as I want it. Make me feel how much you want it."

Sandra climbed on top of me, waiting.

"I want to use both my hands---"

"Yes, yes, Tony."

"And with all my strength---"

Yes, yes, yes, darling."

"I'll lift, and I'll turn."

"And? Sandra smothered me with kisses.

"And I'll listen, and I'll hear---"

"Talk, talk to me, Tony." Sandra was all over my body. "What will you hear, sweetheart?"

"I will hear a gush."

"Oh, yes, I will gush! I will gush with such happiness, Tony."

"I will finally hear the gush of the flush!"

"The flush?" Sandra asked.

"Yes, yes, yes, that flush, that wonderful sound when I can hear the water, flush!"

Sandra jumped up and stared at me.

"That's what you are looking forward too? You want to flush the toilet?" her hands were on her hips. She was indignant.

Laughing, I said. "Come on, let's get out of here and have some fun."

"I don't think so!" She ran off, and I ran after her.

"I don't want to go with you!" She yelled. "Go flush yourself down the toilet!"

"I was only joking, honey. I need to laugh sometimes, too. Come on, what do you say?"

"It's too late. Besides, I'm angry."

"Please, please, please." I kissed the back of her neck and imprisoned her in my arms.

"Hiram is probably sleeping, and the guards are watching their TV programs, so no one is around to take us." She said.

"The hell with them. No guards and no Hiram. Tonight will be ours alone!"

I looked out the window and saw one of the cars in front. "I'll drive myself. We'll find some little place to eat that's not busy and not on the main street. Come on." I pulled Sandra upstairs. "I'm going to dress up, so no one will know me. We're going to have fun!"

We ran upstairs, giggling like two school kids who were going to do something naughty.

Sandra put one of her blonde wigs on me and made up my face. We found a skirt that fit, but I looked like a boy in her sweater, so she made me wear a bra and stuffed it with toilet paper. Then, she found long earrings for me, but I had to wear my own sneakers because her shoes were much too small.

Sandra said I was a very sexy-looking girl, but I tried to kiss her. She ran around the bed laughing and saying I wasn't her type. We had more fun than we had in months.

We went down the huge spiral staircase, slowly and quietly, careful it wouldn't squeak. I found Hiram's car keys in the kitchen drawer where he always kept them and tip-toed out the side door. We looked around and without a sound, sneaked past the guards who were half asleep.

We ran to the car, but I was afraid someone would hear us if I turned on the ignition, so Sandra got in and steered while I pushed the car away from the house, to the front gate. Quickly, I clicked the gate open, got in, and guided the car down the hill. When we're at the safe distance from the house, I turned on the ignition and quickly drove away.

We were thrilled with ourselves and couldn't stop laughing. "Can you believe we out-foxed the Secret Service?"

"That proves how safe we are, Tony."

"I think they just watched that no one gets into the house. They don't expect us to leave."

Sandra sat close to me.

"It feels like we're on a date. They're even playing our song on the radio, Tony. I mean, Tina."

I sang along with the music.

"We're in love, that's amore---"

"I love to hear you sing, Tony. Maybe you could make records and give up your business."

"Let's forget about business tonight, honey."

About an hour later, we saw some lights ahead that turned out to be a small Italian restaurant that was jammed with cars and trucks. I finally found a place to park.

"Tony. Do you think it's safe for us to go in?"

"Sure, no one will know us the way we're dressed. Just remember, my name is Tina. Come on, let's go in. I'm starving!"

It wasn't anything fancy inside, but the food smelled good, and it had a three-piece band.

The hostess came over and led us to a small table at the back of the crowded room. As we passed the bar, a guy smiled at me.

"You're a knockout as a girl. Men are making eyes at you." Sandra teased, as we sat down.

"You order. My voice will never pass as a girl's."

Sandra ordered a bottle of Chianti with dinner, while I just nodded and smiled. We couldn't dance together so we listened to the music and enjoyed our wine with the tasty food. We were in our private heaven.

"It's wonderful when just the two of us are out together without the guards. We have to do it more often, Tony. I don't care if you have curls and lipstick, I still love you."

I was about to kiss her, but I stopped myself in time. "Sandra, I think the wine is dulling my sense. I'm forgetting who I am supposed to be tonight."

"That's because you haven't had a drink for a long time. The doctors don't want you to drink.

"Tonight is different. Tonight is special. I don't care what the doctors say!"

After we finished eating, Sandra jokingly invited me to join her in the lady's room, but I figured I'd be better off doing my business at home.

As I sat there alone, the guy from the bar started eyeing me again. I looked away and stared into my drink until I heard a man's voice next to me.

"I noticed you when you walked in. I'm Joe. I'm here with my friend Fred. Fred's at the bar. See? He's waving. We're alone too. How about us joining you?"

I was afraid of my deep voice, so I shook my head, no. "What's the matter? You don't like me?"

He sounded rough and a little drunk. I had to be a lady. I shook my head, yes.

"Oh, you do like me."

Joe pulled out a chair and sat down beside me.

"You don't know me yet, but everyone likes me. I'm a real nice guy. Why don't you say something?"

I remained silent.

"I won't bite. I noticed you talked plenty when your girlfriend was sitting here. We were watching you. She's a pretty thing too. You're both two good-looking broads."

I kept drinking my wine. I wished Sandra would come back. I was getting nervous especially when he put his face close to mine. I didn't shave too well today.

"That's OK. You don't have to talk. The silent type would be a change. My last wife, she talked and talked and talked. She never shut up! In fact, my three wives all talked a lot. The only time they were quiet was after they were dead!"

Just then, Sandra came to the table, and Joe got up from her chair.

"Hello, pretty lady. I'm Joe. I've been sitting here, talking to your girlfriend but she doesn't talk much. In fact, she doesn't talk at all. Do you talk?"

Joe's friend, Fred, came over from the bar all smiles. He shook our hands and helped Sandra and I looked at each other and start eating our cold spaghetti.

"Your girlfriend is a pretty good eater," Joe said to Sandra. "But she doesn't talk. Won't even tell us your names. What's your name kid?"

"I'm Sandy. My friend's name is Tina."

Sandra stared at her spaghetti curled it around her fork and our eyes met.

"Take your time girls. We ain't in any hurry. We're not goin' anywhere right away. A lady's got to eat." Joe said.

"How come Joe and me never seen you, girls, around here before? I thought we knew all the chicks in this territory. You from around here?"

"Just passing through," Sandra told them.

"Just passing through. You talk nice. You talk like a real lady but sometimes we can't tell a lady from a prostitute."

I sensed trouble. We had to get out of here. Just then, Fred put his arm around Sandra.

"Please don't do that."

"What's the matter, baby? Don't you like me?"

"It's not you. We just don't go for men."

"You mean you're lesbians?"

They stared at us. I was so proud of Sandra. She knew just what to say at the right time.

"I don't believe it! We have been watchin' and you two never touched each other. We don't have anything against lesbians, to each, its own, but I think you're pullin' our legs!" Fred said as he kissed Sandra on the neck.

That was it! I picked up my plate of spaghetti and threw it in Fred's face. Sandra threw her plate into Joe's face and we made a run for the door.

"You bitch!' one yelled.

'You didn't pay your check!" The waitress screamed.

"I'll send it to you!" I shouted as we ran from the restaurant to the parking lot.

"Don't stop running! Just find the car!"

There it was! We climbed in, the doors locked, and—"Where are the keys?"

"You have the keys.

"I don't have them. I gave them to you!"

"Why would you give them to me? I didn't drive!"

I looked in my mirror and saw the guys pick up my wig. "You're a dead man!" One yelled.

"Tony, if they get us, God knows what they'll do!" "I can't find the keys!"

"Look, they're in the ignition!"

We took off just as the two guys jumped into their car and chased after us. I pushed the pedal to the floor, and then it happened.

"Sandra, I need a bathroom!"

"You can't stop! They'll beat you up! They know you're a man!"

We raced through the dark roads. "They're getting closer! Go faster! If they get us, they might kill you!"

I pulled out my wallet. "Here, hold my wallet out the window. When you think they see it, drop it. Maybe they'll stop."

"Wishful thinking, but I'll try." She waved the wallet, but they just honked their horn and yelled.

"You pervert! We'll screw your head off!"

"They don't want money, Tony! They want your head!"

"I need to find a bathroom and a gas station. We're almost on empty!"

"Forget it! Just drive!"

Sandra opened the glove compartment. "There's a gun in here!"

"Great! Shoot it out the window!" I yelled.

"I don't know how to shoot it!"

"Hold it out the window. Maybe it will scare them off."

"Good thinking!" I yelled.

Sandra picked up the gun and looked at it. "I think I should try to shoot it."

She lifted it and put her finger on the trigger.

"Not in the car! Shoot it out the window!" I yelled.

Sandra stuck her hand with the gun out the window and screamed.

"Damn it! I dropped it!"

"Our one chance to protect ourselves, and you had to drop it! Shit!"

"It wasn't my fault! You were driving too fast!"

"You want me to slow down so we get killed?"

Sandra looked out the back window. "Drive faster! They're gaining on us!" she yelled.

We were almost to the house. Another quarter of a mile, and we would get to the last road that led to our property.

I saw men with flashlights and guns walking around. It was the Secret Service looking for us. I yelled.

"It's us! We're being followed!"

I reached the last road that led to the house. The guards called our names.

"Tony, Sandra, are you alright?"

"Open the gates fast! We're being followed!"

The gates immediately opened. I drove through and up the hill to the house, which was ablaze with lights. And Milton was there with two policemen, but as I ran to my office to make a deposit, Hiram, Milton, the policemen, and some of the Secret Service men ran after me.

"Are you all right? What happened? Were you abducted from the house? Who is chasing you?"

I closed my office door in their faces and sighed relief as I sat down. I definitely ate too much, but it would make the government very happy.

Sandra called me, and we watched two police cars chase Fred and Joe's car as it smashed through our gates and crashed into the back of our Lexus.

The guards greeted them with guns, handcuffed them, and took them away.

The phone kept ringing because a reporter heard the police radio message and brought cameramen to our gate. It was a madhouse! Now everyone knew where we lived.

Hiram was angry. "You are in my protective care. I am responsible for you! You should not have left these premises without proper protection! How did you get away without someone seeing you leave?"

Before I had a chance to defend what we did, Milton pulled us into the library.

"Do you two know what could have happened to you? Do you realize what's at stake and how many people rely on you? This is not a joke! It's not funny what you did. You could have been killed!" said Milton.

"It's our life." Sandra told him. "You've mixed into it too much! You don't know how difficult it is to live this way. Sure, we have a lot of material things, and we are famous, but plenty is missing! We had a good time tonight. The best time in months, even if it did end badly!"

With those words, she ran out of the room and upstairs. Milton and I talked into the wee hours of the morning.

"Tony, I'm not going to mince words. You can't let my sister talk you into risking your life. Too many people depend on your miraculous ability. Don't let my sister do to you what Eve did to Adam. The world was punished because he listened to Eve and ate the apple!"

"It wasn't Eve. It was the serpent's fault, Milton."

"We're talking about temptation! Whether it's Eve, the serpent, or my sister.

You have an important full time job with our government, Tony! They need you. If your ability stops by itself, then there is nothing we can do about it. But don't look for trouble!"

Milton stayed the night, and the next day, I listened as he spoke to his sister.

"You have to forget yourself, Sandra. Tony is an important man. He has this job which helps the sick, helps undeveloped countries, and finances medical studies and many, many other things. You should know what is being done with his resources. You get the reports!

If Tony didn't have this ability, and he didn't agree to the government's use of it, the world would not be changing for the better.

Sandra, you are a very important part of this change because Tony needs your love. Without your love, he might not be able to handle all this. It's an enormous responsibility! You need to keep him safe and happy."

Milton talked and talked, but Sandra had her point of view.

"I can't live like this! I know I am selfish, but I want a family. What you call wealth is not what I call wealth, Milton. Gucci doesn't replace sex, and Wall Street isn't a family! I was happy when I worked, ran my own home, and enjoyed being with my family and friends. I felt like I was accomplishing something. Now, I am supposed to sit like a prima donna and do nothing! Sure, I own a gorgeous home, have a chauffeur, and plenty of money, but we are not living. We can't go anywhere. I'm lonely. I need family. I need people."

There was silence. I patted her head and tried to comfort her, but I couldn't calm her down.

"I want my mother to move in!"

"What? Five years I did time in your mother's house. I don't need her aggravation anymore, especially now!" I walked up and down.

"Mother loves you."

"Now? Now she loves me?"

"She would do anything for you, Tony. Whenever I call her on the phone, she tells me she feels like she lost a son. She wouldn't do anything to upset you. She worships the ground you walk on. She's become a different person, a different kind of Mother-in-law."

I stood my ground.

"No! Definitely, N-O!"

Sandra gave me an angry look. "You should have been a priest, and then you could help the world and never have sex!"

"But we wouldn't have married."

"Maybe we should not have married!"

Sandra stormed out of the room, and that night I slept alone in one of our many extra bedrooms.

The following day, a guard who supervised the outside came in to see me.

"We are having trouble at the gate, Mr. Costello. An older woman has pitched a tent there, and she won't leave. She has brought TV cameramen, and she's giving them interviews. She claims she's your Mother-in-law."

"Sandra!"

I screamed through the halls of the house.

"Sandra!"

She finally came down the stairs.

"What are you yelling about?"

I dragged her by the hand into the den where the TV showed her mother, big as life, being interviewed in front of our gates, as cars drove up, parked, and watched Vera cry into her handkerchief and moan into the speaker.

"My Antonio, such a wonderful Son-in-law he is. In such a mansion, he lives. Wings like a bird, his mansion has. In such a place, invisible a Mother-in-law could be.

So much I miss how we lived together with Harmony---- mine cat. Also with my daughter he lived and with free rent in mine house he lived.

Now, alone, cold in mine tent I stay, but warm in mine heart I feel, and so close to my children I am. Only one Mother-in-law he has."

The cameras had a field day. Sandra ran outside to her mother, and they both sobbed on each other's shoulders on national TV.

I was the ogre! I told the guard, who was in the room with me, to wipe his eyes and bring them both inside.

That was the day Vera moved in. Leave it to her. She had a moving van waiting down the road with all her possessions, and she had already rented her apartment in Brooklyn. I was up the creek! Che macello! (What a mess!)

From the day Vera moved in, things began to go wrong. Now everyone knew where we lived, so the guards had a hard time keeping people off our land. Although no one could get through our gates, many tried to climb over them, and the helicopters from Washington had problems landing and taking off.

Then I began to have trouble in my office, and it became worse day by day. My moment of horror was when I couldn't work at all. I became completely dysfunctional. I was out of business!

I didn't want to blame it on Vera. She tried very hard to be nice to me. She kissed me, hugged me, and wished on me all kinds of things in Yiddish. Sandra said they were good things.

I disappointed my business partner, the U.S. government. The President's secretary called every day with the same advice.

"Send your Mother-in-law packing!"

I knew I couldn't do that because Sandra was happy with her mother living here.

Every day I disappeared into the solitude of my wonderful home office where I sat and watched TV, used my exercise equipment, turned on my stereo, and took a relaxing bath, but nothing helped.

I couldn't sleep, so I walked the floor all night. Sandra kept asking me what was wrong, but I didn't want to tell her. Eventually, to get a night's sleep, she went to her mother's room.

The next day the women went shopping together in disguise, and I was left to spend the day watching nothing happen.

I called Milton.

"I can't do it anymore. It's over. The miracle is over! What should I do?"

"Relax. Don't get upset. That's the worst thing you can do. I'll speak to the other doctors."

"But Brinks is coming to collect, and I won't have anything for them!"

"It will happen. I'll call later."

I sat in my office waiting, waiting, and waiting. Milton kept calling with advice from the doctors about which medicines to take. I tried everything they suggested but nothing worked. What was I going to do? I needed to keep this business going. This would be a terrible time for the government to lose me! Besides, I loved being rich!

Amelia made me special ice cream floats with prune juice, and Hiram had me nibbling on licorice while listening to my piped-in music. Then, right there on the job, I fell asleep until I heard voices calling. The happy campers were home.

"Come out and see what we found in the stores, Tony." I came out very reluctantly.

"Look what we bought, honey."

"I thought you said you found them."

"Only an expression, dear, but we did find bargains."

Vera gave me a big kiss and sprayed me with something called Fiji In Summer. I learned that a tiny bottle of perfume cost me twelve hundred dollars. It didn't even smell good, but Sandra said her mother wanted it, and whatever Vera wants, Vera gets.

Sandra danced around while she helped Hiram bring in the bags and boxes from Bergdorf, Neiman Marcus, Louis Vuitton, Cartier, and others. It was Christmas in July, and I was Santa Claus. My wife was happy. What a pity to put an end to all this.

"Look at Mother's beautiful Gucci sunglasses. Doesn't she look like a movie star?"

"Just like a movie star. I hear Hollywood calling her. I bet if she went to Hollywood, they would grab her. I could fix it for you, Vera. I have connections. What do you say?"

"Hollywood? Do you think in Hollywood, I should be? I think maybe too skinny they would make me. Toothpicks, in Hollywood, live.

Only toothpicks they want."

"Why would Mother want to leave us? She has everything she needs right here." Sandra smiled as she showed me the two Rolex watches she bought.

"One for Mother and one for me."

"What about me?" I asked.

"You never liked clothes or jewelry, remember?"

"I never had money to buy any before. Things have changed." I said.

"For you, we will pick out next time. Maybe clothes you need for going to the White House? Armani, next time we bring you, Armani." Vera promised.

"Look, honey, Prada had their fur bags on sale. Only fourteen hundred, so I bought six.

"Fourteen hundred for six pocketbooks? That's no bargain!"

"Each one fourteen hundred it was. Mine daughter, one hundred dollars she saved you on each bag because off-season it is."

"Look at this beautiful little chinchilla bag, Tony. Isn't it adorable?"

Sandra walked back and forth, modeling it.

"How adorable was the baby chinchilla that gave up its life to become a bag?" I asked.

"It was probably an old chinchilla that was about to die." She answered.

"They use baby animals because the fur is softer, Sandra. What other dead baby animals did you bring home as bags?"

"You're being mean, Tony. If I didn't buy them, someone else would. I'm not going to return the bags. The animals are already dead!"

Sandra was very angry. Her dark eyes became darker when she was angry. She really got me going when she looked this way. "I'm ashamed of you, Sandra."

"Do you really think they are babies, Tony?" Sandra asked.

"A Jewish guilt trip on my daughter you shouldn't put!"

"You could return the bags and contribute the money to, Save the Animals Organization." I suggested.

"I don't know what to do. You've upset me, Tony!"

I watched as Hiram, Amelia, two guards, and my happy campers schlepped (pulled) their packages upstairs. Vera was rubbing off on me. I was beginning to speak Yiddish. Now I had to explain to the big spenders what was happening to my business in a language they could both understand.

A few days later, finances were no better and I had to say something. In a dream, it came to me. I remembered that special word my Mother-in-law used just before our wedding.

"I have tzores. (troubles) My business is of tzores!" I told them.

"You mean maybe out of business you could be?" Vera asked.

"Yes. You may have to schlep all those things back. We may have to sell this house that we bought and everything that goes with it!"

Vera became emotionally upset. She started screaming to Sandra.

"Go, quickly, Milton, you should call! Go! Why you don't call?"

I told Vera, "Milton already knows, and we are just waiting to see what will happen."

"What will happen? Nothing maybe will happen, and what will we do? Who could give up such a lifestyle?" Vera complained.

"What will I be giving up, Mama? A lifestyle of shopping for trinkets? A cold and empty house with too many bedrooms? A husband that is still a virgin?" Sandra asked.

Vera suggested, "Maybe from your body onions he should eat."

"We tried that, Mama. We cried from the onions during the whole picnic." I said.

"Raw onions may be used. First, the onions you cook!"

"I don't want Milton to help Tony." Sandra was very serious. "Maybe now, Tony will get better without an operation, and we will have children and a real-life!"

"Crazy you talk! You only want your stomach should swell like a mountain from babies! Dumkop (Dumbbell), a puppy you should buy!"

Vera ran to the phone. "Milton, I will call. Such a life who throws away?"

Vera spoke to Milton for quite a while and then turned to us with tears trickling down her cheeks.

"My son, he says maybe spoiling things I am for you, so I should go. So I go."

"No! You have to stay, Mama. I want you to stay."

Sandra put her arms around Vera and kissed her. Vera started to cry, and Sandra yelled at me.

"This is your entire fault!"

"I couldn't believe it. She blamed me for what? I didn't tell her mother to leave. I thought she was happy because I was losing my power. I had it! I needed a drink. I went into the library, poured myself a large glass of scotch, and thought about my future.

What if I had lost my ability? I had another drink. I wanted things to continue the way they were, but it seemed everything was going to change. I felt very depressed. I poured myself another drink as Sandra came in.

"Tony, I'm sorry I blamed you."

She came over and kissed me. "You've been drinking! You're not supposed to drink."

"What do you care? You don't want me to be able to do it anymore, anyway."

"I couldn't live with myself if I made you lose your gift,

Tony. If Mother's living with us is causing these problems, I'll get her an apartment elsewhere."

"It doesn't matter anymore. I don't think anything is going to help. I don't want to talk about it. I'm exhausted. I'm going to bed."

The next day Sandra said I hit her while I was sleeping. "I'm upset, so you better not sleep with me." I said.

"Tony, you hit me accidentally. It's probably from your drinking. I don't want to stop sleeping together. I love you, Tony. Please stop drinking."

"I sleep better when I'm alone. I want to be alone!"

Sandra came over to me and put her hand on mine. I pushed it away.

"Tony, I love you. Why are you torturing yourself and me? It's not the end of the world if you can't do it anymore."

"It's the end of my world!" I said as I poured myself another scotch.

"You don't understand me. You never understood me; all my life, people have helped me, and now I want to help them. I was able to do this. I was happy doing it. Now, it's all over. I'm finished!"

"You need the psychiatrist. I'm calling him to come over."

"Don't you dare! If you want to help me, get off my back!" Sandra didn't say anything. I turned away and went upstairs to my bedroom with my bottle.

I could not accept what was happening to me; I never went a week without producing. The pressure was getting to me. I knew Milton should take me to the hospital but I hated that place. I wanted to run away from everything, so I lay down and drank myself into oblivion.

It was dark in my room when I heard my bedroom door open.

"I called Milton. He's coming over!" Sandra announced and then left.

I finished the rest of the scotch and fell into another stupor. From far away I heard a voice. I thought I was dreaming.

"Tony, Tony, wake up. Milton's here."

"My head felt like someone battered it with a lead pipe. I was freezing. I shivered from the cold. I opened my eyes, but the light hurt them. "Shut the lights!" I yelled.

"The lights aren't on, Tony."

"Who's there?"

"It's me, Tony. It's Milton. How do you feel?'

He put his hand on my forehead.

"You're very hot. You have a fever."

"I'm going to vomit!" I said as I tried to lift myself up and go to the toilet, but I couldn't make it. I threw up all over the bed.

Sandra picked up the empty bottle of scotch.

"He's been drinking for two days, Milton."

"Tony, that's no way to solve a problem."

"I don't have a problem. I'm free as a bird. No responsibilities anymore. Soon, Sandra will divorce me because she can't afford Gucci clothes and…"

"Tony, I never wanted Gucci! I only want you!"

"You say that now but when you don't have Gucci, you will miss Gucci!"

"Tony, you are drunk, and you are sick with a fever."

"I won't go to that hospital again!" "It's the best place for you, Tony." Sandra said.

"That hospital is a crazy place. Things happened to me in there that were very strange. They let crazy people come in and roam around and attack the patients and…"

"Honey, you don't know what you're saying."

"Ok, Tony, you don't have to go to the hospital, but you have to take your medicine and have a nurse stay with you."

"I don't want a nurse! She may not be a real nurse. She could be posing as a nurse. She could be an evil nurse. She could be evil, Evelyn!"

"What is he talking about, Milton?

"He's delirious. Don't listen."

I felt a sharp needle in my arm, and then I guess I conked out because the next thing I remember is opening my eyes and seeing my wife sitting next to me, holding a cold compress on my forehead.

"Feeling better?"

"I have to go."

"You have to stay in bed. Your fever was very, very high."

"My stomach hurts. It feels strange."

I ran to my office, my wonderful home away from home. My private domain. A place where people do things they don't do anywhere else.

Then, slowly, very, very slowly, it began. Oh, it felt so good. So very, very good. Oh yes! Yes! Yes! Yes! I was in business again!!!!

"Are you all right?" Sandra called.

"I'm wonderful! I'm great!"

I opened the door and came out smiling from ear to ear. I pulled Sandra to me.

"We've got another piece of the rock!"

"I'm happy if you're happy, Tony."

"Your Mother can stay. She didn't cause my trouble.
"I know. It was a virus."

Vera came over and kissed me.

"Okay, dokay you are?"

"I'm okay dokay now, but I've been thinking. What if I was seriously ill? What if I died?"

"Oh, stop it, Tony. I don't want to think about that."

"We have to think about it because we all have to go some time."

"Going, I'm not!"

"No? How will you manage that, Vera?"

"Refusing I am to go."

"We have to arrange things, Sandra."

"What things?"

"Burial for you and me, in your family cemetery."

"Mother, don't you have a plot next to Dad's?"

"If a plot there I had, already there I would be. Anyplace he would go, always he schlepped me."

"Mother, be sensible. Wives are buried next to their husbands."

"I'll buy you a plot next to your husband, Vera."

"If I should decide to go, only next to you both I am going! Together we will all go!"

"No, Vera! I want to be alone with my wife!" I stood my ground.

"Mother, why do you want to be next to us in the cemetery?"

"My heart tells me, God gives Tony such a gift when he lives, maybe when the pearly gates open a better one he gets. So long I'm going to schlep!

Besides, in mine liberal, reform Jewish cemetery, I want for sure you get in."

"We won't have trouble, Mother. We know people of different religions that are there."

"Already God knows such a good person, Tony, you are. So many mitzvahs (good deeds) you do. Maybe front row in the temple you don't sit but, like a chazzan (cantor), you sing. And so much chopped liver you eat! Even to the borscht circuit (Catskills Jewish hotels), you went. Almost an Italian Jew you are. But maybe, before you go, the blessing over the bread you should learn."

"I already know the blessing over the wine."

I sang the prayer that I heard dozens of times and surprised them both.

"My Tony, you sound like a Jewish Dean Martin.", Sandra said.

"No, no, no, like my Perry Como, he sounds." Vera insisted.

"Don't fight over me, girls. I'm already a commercial commodity."

Well, it was settled. I would purchase three plots next to each other. We would all be together even after death, do us part. The next day Milton insisted I needed a new psychiatrist who could help me relax since Vera was staying.

"But what happened wasn't Mother's fault!" Sandra insisted.

"Not this time," Milton replied. "Just listen to me, both of you. It's an insurance policy on your future."

Now, Dr. Abramowitz comes to our home twice a week. He is a middle-aged man who has worked with NASA and all the men who went up into space.

He told me he's worked with many famous artists like Jackson Pollock.

He said he helped him with his drinking problem and worked with him for many years.

He seems to understand how people are always expecting more from gifted people and the pressure it creates. He understands the burden of being a celebrity.

He believes I need changes in my lifestyle and environment, so he had my office painted brown and told me to concentrate on that color and listen to the music of Brahms and Chopin while I work.

He explained that I must have complete peace of mind in my office so he had my desk and telephone removed and some Monet paintings put on the walls.

He said nothing should excite me while I am in there so I am only allowed to watch certain programs on TV. He said, 'The Sopranos' is off-limits, and he wants a juice bar put in immediately.

As the months go by, under the tutelage of the doctor and the sad elimination of the three things I love; coffee, cheese, and 'The Sopranos', I've become a regular businessman.

Sandra tries to make up for the things in life she doesn't have by shopping more. She and Vera made shopping into an art form. All the furniture that came with the house has disappeared, and new, expensive furnishings arrive each day with the help of our decorator.

The girls found themselves a very expensive and popular decorator. He is a tiny, skinny man with a black Van Dyke beard, who wears a smile, tight, black, leather leotards, and a shirt that floats in the air as he flutters through our home on his tippy toes. Everyone adores him.

His name is Tito Ginsberg. He is a Chinese Jew who comes from Mexico. His influence throughout our house looks to me like a mishmash of garbage no one knew what to do with, but I'm told it's eclectic and gorgeous. Now Sandra wants our friends and relations to visit.

"1 want a house-warming! I want people to see what success has done for us. I want them to see the showplace of a gifted celebrity!"

Everyone warned us it was too dangerous to have a party, but Sandra didn't want to listen. Even Vera told her to forget it, and she did, forget it, for an hour.

"We will have extra guards, and everyone will show their invitation at the gate. Then we can have them checked again before they come in our front door. What could possibly go wrong?" she asked.

It sounded like it would be OK, so I discussed it with Hiram, who wasn't too happy about it.

"I don't think it's wise. Many things can go wrong. It could be very dangerous."

"But my wife insists! That's all she talks about. She's driving me crazy!"

"It's not good for you to get upset over this, Tony. Maybe we could arrange a small party, but I must be the one to plan it so that everything is made as safe as possible. The important thing is that we keep the party small. Not more than twenty people can be invited."

Sandra sent out her invitations, but when the RSVP's came back, over a hundred people were coming to our open house. Hiram hit the roof!

"I became mixed up between couples and people," Sandra said. "That would only make forty people, Madam Sandra!" Hiram responded.

"I can't tell them not to come. It's too late! Just hire more guards." Sandra insisted.

A month later, on a Sunday afternoon at five o'clock, cars started to arrive outside our gates. We watched on our TV as the guards parked each car and checked the invitations.

Then the guests were seated in a little trolley and driven up the hill to our front door, and carefully screened again before they entered the house.

Couples arrived who we had been friends with since we were married, but most of them were Sandra's relatives I never met, Vera's friends I never met and Sandra's co-workers that I never met.

Sandra's cousins, Hymie, Isaac, and Jacob, gave us a cute little Shiatsu dog for a house gift.

We thanked them and explained no animals were allowed in our home because the doctors were afraid their business and my business could get mixed up.

Jack, a friend, came in with the latest 'Butt' magazine. The cover was full of butts with my face in the middle.

Vera, bedecked, in a beaded ball gown, which I learned cost me twelve thousand dollars, welcomed everyone to Sandra's home and then, as an afterthought, including my name.

My wife layered in diamonds, with newly capped teeth that glowed when she smiled, illuminated the room like a chandelier.

The guards, dressed as waiters, walked around with trays of hors d'oeuvres while other plainclothes men passed as bartenders.

The liquor flowed but not in my direction. I was watched very carefully. When Vera saw me with a drink, she pulled it from my hand.

"You want it should kill your business?" She asked as she drank it down.

Milton introduced us to the beautiful girl he was living with as Vera whispered,

"Broomstick number three, she's here!"

The six-piece band and singer sounded great, but they were very carefully watched by Hiram, who learned, too late, their references didn't check out.

Sandra's old girlfriends from high school came with their husbands but one came along. Her name was Iris and she was gorgeous. I mean really drop-dead gorgeous! She told me her husband was dead and she was very unhappy living alone. She attached herself to me right away. It didn't take long before Vera pulled me aside.

"Too much you look at her boom-booms. Real, they're not! Real, nothing is! Plastic she is. The plastic surgeon takes her dead husband's money, then plastic her face and body he makes."

Vera ran off to pull Hiram on the dance floor as Iris glided towards me; her long, red, gorgeous hair cascaded down over her almost bare, plastic breasts. She was enticed to look at me as she took my hand and tried to lure me to the dance floor.

"You can't refuse your wife's oldest and dearest friend a dance, can you?"

I could feel Sandra's eyes follow us as we danced. Iris held me very tight, and her full red lips kept brushing against mine. "Is there someplace we can be alone?" She whispered in my ear.

"Not really."

"You're breaking my heart." She pouted.

"You're crazy!"

"Crazy about you."

"My wife is watching." We stopped dancing, and I walked off the dance floor as Iris followed me.

"What if your wife wasn't watching?" She asked in a low Marilyn Monroe voice as she took a long drag on a cigarette.

"We don't smoke here."

"You begrudge me one little cigarette?" She questioned as she blew smoke in my face.

Sandra glared at me. I smiled back. She knew she had nothing to worry about. What was I capable of doing?

The music stopped. Sandra came over to us, and without saying a word, she took my hand and pulled me down the hall.

"Who was that?"

"She's your friend."

"She's not a friend of mine. What's her name?"

"I don't know. I think it's the name of a flower, like Rose or Daisy."

"I think she's a hooker! I think there's a hooker in my house!"

Sandra raised her voice. She began to scream. She sounded drunk. I never saw her like this before."

"There's a hooker here! A hooker in my house!"

Suddenly one of the male entertainers came over to us. "We need you on the dance floor, both of you, right now!"

He took our hands and led us into the other room where the drums beat and the singers stood on stage and sang to me. "Thank you. We just want to thank you.

You're a wonderful person. A person of who we are proud. Bless you. We bless you and love you. Love you for just being you. Wonderful, wonderful you."

They sang the song a few times, then friends pulled us on the dance floor, and everyone joined us to dance.

A few minutes later, I looked up to see my very, very old minister friend, Dr. Murray, take the microphone. I was afraid he had a little too much to drink, so I went and stood next to him. The band stopped playing.

"1 have something very important to say about this wonderful, young man, Tony.

This poor boy from humble beginnings came to me in a time of need. Now, this same young man, out of the goodness of his heart, helps those in need."

Everyone applauded and yelled my name. Dr. Murray raised his hand and then continued.

"Thousands of years ago, the builders of the pyramids foresaw the future in the formation of the stars.

Abraham, Joseph, and Moses were also astronomers who foretold the future in their days.

Centuries later, famous astronomers, mathematicians, philosophers, and physicists like Copernicus, Newton, and Galileo told what they saw in the heavens, and most of it agreed with the early builders of the pyramids, but much of it was rejected in their lifetime by those with authority.

All the famous men believed that the celestial bodies of the heavens governed life on earth.

They believed that once in every trillion years, there would come to earth one celestial aberration, a heavenly body that would deviate from the normal or expected course.

This aberration has occurred here with our beloved Tony, who uses his gift to benefit all mankind.

I raise my glass to Tony. A beloved, kind, and generous human being. May he continue to be our source of hope."

Everyone applauded, but then my old and good friend continued.

"I want to add that if I can ever do anything for you, Tony, I am here.

If you're ever in need of a liver transplant, I am here. Blood also. Blood is here too. I have it.

I think tonight we should all sign up to give our help to Tony if ever he is in need.

Remember, it isn't always what Tony can do for our country but also what our country can do for Tony!

So, liver transplants line up and sign in the left aisle. Heart transplants on the right and blood donors sign here in the middle."

"No, no, this is not necessary!" I said on the microphone as everyone went to sign up.

We helped old Dr. Murray to a seat as he kissed my hand. "You are the divine spirit sent to us from the heavens."

I didn't feel very divine, especially after staring at Iris's boobs all night but maybe that pleasure was God's way of saying, 'Keep up the good work!'

It was after one thirty a.m. before everyone finally left. The guards opened up the second floor, which had been roped off, so we could go to bed.

Vera passed out on a couch, and since no one wanted to carry her little fat body up the winding stairway, Amelia put her to bed in her bedroom downstairs.

Sandra looked inebriated as she walked up the stairs, but when I tried to help her, she pushed me away.

"Wasn't it a perfectly marvelous party with all those friends, new friends, my friends?" She asked as she swung her arms forward and pushed open our bedroom door so it banged against the wall.

"It was a great party Sandra; however, I think you drank too much."

I tried to help her get into bed, but she resisted me and fell on her face.

"You looked like you really enjoyed the party!" She said as she threw her shoe at me.

"Take it easy, Sandra. You had too much to drink." I sat down next to her in bed, but she stood up.

"That girl was all over you tonight! I mean literally all over you! Everyone was watching! You made a fool of me and yourself!"

"I tried to get away from Iris but"

"Oh, so you do remember her name!"

"Will you ever let me forget it?"

"You said she was like a flower!"

"No! No! I said her name was a flower, like cauliflower or poison ivy. I couldn't get away from her. She followed me and pulled me on the dance floor. I couldn't get away!"

"I bet!"

"She is your friend and was our guest, so I had to be nice to her. Besides, she just lost her husband."

"Lost? She lost him all right. He probably died of mysterious circumstances. Do you know that the authorities questioned if she killed him?

Her husband probably acted like you did tonight with some bimbo, so she did away with him." Sandra climbed under the covers.

"You wouldn't do something like that." I got into bed next to her.

"Don't be too sure." She turned her head away from me. "Don't blame me. You invited her!"

"I didn't know she went through a complete overhauling and came out looking like that!"

"It's amazing what plastic surgery can do." I said. "I think I'll go have plastic surgery."

"Good! Whatever makes you happy?" I turned over and closed my eyes.

"Oh, so you think I need to be done over!" Sandra sat up in bed.

"No!" I insisted. "I don't think you need anything done. I didn't think you needed your teeth capped!"

"Well, now I am going to spend your money faster than you can make it! You'll need to work morning, noon, and night because I'm going for a nose job, a tummy tuck and breast implants! Big, big breast implants so men will stare at them as you stared at hers! Do you hear me?"

"I hear you, but you don't need to do all that. I love you just the way you are." I shut off the light and patted her bottom.

"I love my wife, my wonderful wife, my beautiful wife, my gorgeous wife. I want to hold my wife." I moved closer to her. "I want to kiss my wife."

I kissed her cheek, her forehead, her nose, and her neck. I snuggled closer to her, and I began to fall asleep.

"I feel a draft from the windows. Go close them." She said. "The windows are closed." I mumbled.

"There is a draft. I hear the wind."

"Maybe it was me snoring."

"No. It's a different noise."

"Maybe it was you snoring."

"I don't snore! Go check the windows!" I pushed off the covers, sat up, and started to reach for the lamp on my night table when I heard something fall on the other side of the room. "Who's there? Is there a guard in our bedroom?"

Sandra sat up. "Your guards are making me sick! Don't you ever go home?"

Again I stretched out my arm to switch on my bedside lamp. "I can't find the damn switch!" I yelled.

All of a sudden, a light shined in my face.

Two masked men stood over us, holding guns and flashlights. "Holy shit!" I yelled.

XII

Sandra started to scream, but her mouth was quickly covered by a large, gloved hand.

"We don't want you, lady, just him, so keep your mouth shut if you want to live!"

"We better take her too." The big one said.

"But Boss, you said we were only taking him."

"I don't care what I said before. I changed my mind. Now cut to the chase!"

"Please, don't take my wife. Leave her here. She can't identify you."

"We need her help with the cooking."

"I never cook. I don't know how to cook. My mother always did the cooking."

"Let's get the Mother."

"She died a long time ago." I said.

"I'm warning you two, if you give us any trouble you got short lives! See these guns? 'They have silencers on them, and they kill real quiet." Boss whispered, as the little guy opened a bag and took out a bottle marked chloroform, and a roll of tape, and tied my hands, feet, and mouth.

"You, Dumhead! How's he going to breathe in the chloroform with a taped mouth?"

"I'll untape. I'll untape, Boss."

He quickly pulled off the tape from my mouth, and as I groaned, the Boss whispered, "Listen, you two, if there is one yell, you're both dead meat!"

"Hey Boss, look at the Rolex."

The little guy picked up my watch and admired it. "We're not here for jewelry, Dumhead, just them!"

"Take whatever you want," I said. "Just leave us alone."

"Take my husband's Armani suits. You're his size so they will fit you. See, there's one on the chair. They are expensive, but you can have them. He has a whole closet full."

"We don't want suits," Boss said.

"Take my wife's Prada bags for your girlfriends."

"No! Not my Prada bags!" Sandra begged.

"We don't want things, only you. Get that through your heads!" Boss said as he took my Rolex away from the little guy and stuck it in his pocket.

"I like your shiny white teeth, lady."

"You can't have them. They don't come out."

"Shut up, Dumhead, and get the chloroform ready. Remember, just enough to knock them out. We don't want to kill them yet."

"We have a vault in the closet, and it's loaded with jewelry and cash. You can have it all. The key is over there." I pointed to the drawer.

Suddenly, the little guy put a cloth filled with chloroform against my face as I bit his wrist with my teeth.

"Shit!" he screamed. Boss quickly muffled the scream with his hand, then shook his gun in my face.

"Don't shoot! Please don't shoot my husband. We'll give you anything you want, anything. You just have to name it. We are very rich, so you can have whatever you want."

"We know you're rich, and we know why you're rich.

Dumhead, we can't waste any more time let's get them out of here."

"I ain't putting my hand near his mouth again!"

"Here, give me the damn chloroform!" Boss said.

"You better think twice before you kidnap us because you will get a life when they catch you! Just take our jewels and money, and we'll forget the whole thing." I said.

Boss pushed the cloth with chloroform against my face as Sandra started to scream, but Dumhead quickly chloroformed her.

"Just so you should know, we won't take anything but you guys. We can't be bought. We don't take pay-offs. We have laws, and we obey them. You got a problem with that?"

I tried to fight the feeling of weakness, but as I took a last look at Sandra, barely conscious, the room swirled, and everything went black.

When I woke up, I didn't know where I was or remember what happened.

I looked around and saw I was in a large, dirty, dark room that appeared to be a living room with cots, couches, chairs, and a TV. Sandra was next to me, unconscious and we were both tied to chairs with our mouths taped.

Next to us was a bathroom, then a kitchen, and there were other rooms down a hall. Blinds covered the windows, so I didn't know if it was day or night.

I partially closed my eyes and pretended I was still knocked out while I watched and listened to our kidnapper's talk.

It seemed three guys were holding us captive, Boss, a tall, dark-haired guy with shifty eyes, Dumhead, short with large ears that stuck out, and a chubby, black fellow they called Louie The Lip.

"Hey." I felt a whack on my head.

"You ain't sleepin. I saw you were lookin at us before."

Boss walked around me. "Don't try and be a wise guy or a hero. I'm gonna warn you just this once, otherwise, your wife will suffer.

We know what you're all about and what you can do for us. You're a very important person, Tony boy. You got a special talent. You're a celebrity. Our kidnapping you are on all the news channels, but they don't know it was us."

Boss turned on the T.V. It showed the stock market hitting a new low and the oil and gold plunging. They blamed it on my disappearance. There was a five million dollar reward to whoever came forward with information about our whereabouts, and search parties were looking everywhere for us.

The phone rang, and Louie answered it.

"It's for you, Boss. It's, The Man."

Boss took the phone into the other room so I couldn't hear much except the name, Manhamen.

When he came back in the room, he said, "I just got a call from, The Man. He says you gotta give us what we want or you and the wife got a short life. Now I'm gonna take off the tape from your mouths, and you can yell all you want cause nobody will hear you cause there ain't any people near this old building."

He pointed to Sandra, who had just woken up.

"If you scream--- and I hate screamin broads, I will tape your mouth shut permanently!"

They removed the tapes with one big yank as Sandra cried, "You big apes, the police will find us, and you'll all go to prison for life!"

"Shut up, you stupid broad," Boss said.

"Don't talk to her like that!" I yelled.

"We'll talk anyway we want to her and do whatever we want to her unless you give us what we want."

"What if I can't give you what you want? What if I can't defecate?"

"We don't know nothin' about this defecate business. We just want you should shit!"

"My material is no good to you. It has to be put through a very sophisticated process by people who are educated in this type of operation. Otherwise, what I have is worthless."

"The Man, he got those connections. He got people to process what you got, but we gotta get the stuff, or we ain't gonna get paid. Now, we are gonna help you do what you gotta do, so all of us can go do what we wanna do."

"Sometimes, I just can't do it! This happens frequently." I said.

"Sometimes it's his emotions that stop it." Sandra said.

"Sometimes it's the food I eat."

"Well, we're gonna keep you here till we get it!"

"Sometimes nothing works," Sandra said. "Once he went for days without producing anything.

"We ain't in any rush. We got plenty of time. Course the big boss, The Man, doesn't like to wait. He and his entire bunch are killers! If they don't get what they want, there ain't no sayin what can happen in this country.

You got yourself mixed up in a big professional operation. The Man, he's mixed up in a deadly operation and we gotta do what they want, or none of us will see daylight again. They will make our lives a livin hell. We are all in big trouble if we don't get what they want from you!

Here Dumhead, take this two hundred dollars and go get food for Tony boy so he can do it."

"How do I know what food gets him to do it?"

"We gotta make a list." Boss said. "Now, in plain talk, Mr. Tony, what makes it happen?"

"It's different every day. Sometimes I eat things, and they work for me, and sometimes nothing works."

"Will you let us go if Tony gives you what you want?" Sandra asked Boss as she made out the shopping list.

"Sure, we'll let you both go right after he supplies us with what The Man wants."

He handed Dumhead the list.

"Now get out of here. Go get food!"

Dumhead started to run out the door as Sandra yelled.

"Don't forget White Cloud! He only uses White Cloud tissues. He has to be made comfortable, or he has problems."

While we waited, they untied me from the chair and walked me over to my dirty throne, where they tied one arm to the sink and the other arm to the cabinet door handle.

"How can I do it all tied up like this?"

"Try. Give it your best shot. Talk to it. Make it listen." They sat outside my throne room and kept their eyes glued to me, the TV news, and Sandra.

Boss kept sending Louie in to see if I made any progress.

"I'm low man on the totem pole, so I always get to do the shitty jobs! Bend over so I can take a look."

"That's what my mother used to say when I was very little. I remember her words. 'Bend over, Tony; I have to take a look.' I don't remember much about her, but lately, those words stand out in my mind." I said.

"I don't remember my mama ever lookin, but with nine kids, how many times can ya look?" Louie took a peek.

"Boss ain't gonna like this. Maybe you are hungry. You got to eat when the food comes, or Boss will use a torpedo to get you goin."

"What you two talkin about in there?" Boss yelled.

"I'm tryin to talk him into doin somethin. They don't call me Louie the Lip for nothin'."

About an hour later, I heard a car drive into the yard. Louie ran outside and helped Dumhead carry in bags and bags of food.

"Do I smell Chinese?" Boss asked as he pulled open the bags. "Chinese was not on the list!"

"But I like Chinese." Dumhead said.

"I don't care what you like!" Boss answered.

"Everybody likes Chinese, Boss. Louie, you like Chinese?"

"I love Chinese. What if Tony The Tongue doesn't like Chinese?" Louie asked.

Dumbhead said, "If he doesn't like it, I'll eat his share."

"You moron! You stupid, nut head of a fool!" Boss hit Dumhead with his fist.

"We don't need you to eat! We need him to eat!"

"But I'm hungry!" Dumbhead cried.

"Soon, I'll give you your eyeballs to eat!" Boss raised a switch-blade to Dumbhead's face. "Now shut up and put the food out!"

Louie untied us, and we walked into the kitchen.

"Chinese food doesn't always work for Tony, but we eat it.", Sandra said.

"He's gonna eat, all right. He's gonna eat like never before!" Boss said.

We sat around the dirty kitchen table, Sandra on one end and me on the other. In every room they separated us so we couldn't talk.

Louie filled a huge platter with Chinese food and placed it in front of me.

"Remember Tony, the more you eat, the more you make, and the quicker you and the misses get out of here. OK?"

"OK. OK.", I said.

All eyes followed me as I continually filled my fork, lifted it into my mouth, and chewed. I kept eating, and they kept staring at me.

"I thought you were all hungry. Why don't you eat?" I asked.

"We're waitin for the magic to happen."

"It takes a while before my bells ring and my fireworks go off." I said.

They began to put food in their mouths, but they kept their eyes glued to me. When I finished one platter, they filled up another one.

"I'm full. I can't eat anymore."

"How about some spare ribs? Some more shrimp? It's good you didn't eat the rice. It could stop you from doin it." Louie said.

"How did you find out that, Louie? You've been readin them books again?" Dumhead asked.

Everyone finished eating, but they kept sitting around the table waiting, waiting, waiting.

"Well?" Boss asked.

"Anything happenin?" Dumhead asked.

Sandra's worried look convinced me to eat some of the second platters.

"I'll walk ya over to the throne." Louie offered.

"I don't feel anything, not yet."

"Not yet?" The guys asked in unison.

"Soon." I told them.

"Soon." They smiled hopefully.

"I'm gonna read your fortune cookie, Tony boy." Boss said as he broke it open.

"It says, 'He who has sore ass gathers a lifetime of longevity."

"What's that mean?" Dumbhead asked.

"It means if Tony gets his ass sore from his work, God will reward him with a long life."

"How you always know so much, Boss? You must read lots of books. One day, I'm gonna read a book."

"Prunes!" Boss shouted. "Go Dumhead, here are fifty dollars. Go get prunes!"

Dumhead left, and Louie started feeding me more Chinese food. "Do you feel it yet?"

"I feel like I'm going to throwup."

"You mustn't throw up, Tony. Try to do it the way they want you to." Sandra said as she turned to Boss and asked.

"Let me talk to my husband privately. It might help."

He let Sandra move next to me, and we whispered softly to one another.

"You need to give them something, Tony. We have to get out of here!"

"You think I want to stay? What makes you think they will let us go when I give them something?" I whispered.

"You mean they will never let us go?"

"Would you let a money-making machine go?"

"Tony, you're a person, not a machine!"

"These thugs work for terrorists who don't care what I am."

"I'm so scared, Tony."

"I'm sorry, Sandra. It's my fault you're here. If I listened to you and had that operation, none of this would have happened."

"Don't blame yourself, Tony. Let's just think of how we can get out of here."

The sound of squeaking brakes filled the room, and Louie ran out to help carry the boxes of prunes into the room.

"Where do we put 'ern?" Dumhead asked.

"Where do you think?" Boss yelled.

Louie and Dumhead lined up the boxes in front of me as I counted them. There were twenty-five boxes of prunes.

"Now what?" Dumhead asked.

"Open them!" Boss screamed.

Both guys madly tore open the boxes. One by one, I started to eat as everyone watched me.

"They have pits!" I said.

"You bought prunes with pits? What if he chokes on a pit?" Boss lifted Dumhead by the hair.

"I didn't know prunes was without pits, honest, Boss."

"Prunes are like people. Some prunes have pits, and some people have brains. Now take out all the pits, Dumhead!"

"You want I should take out all the pits with my fingers?"

I looked at Dumhead's dirty fingers.

"Don't worry. I'll be careful. I never swallowed a pit yet."

I continued eating. Everyone was very watchful in case I didn't spit out the pit. They brought me a special bowl just for pits and counted each pit as I spit it into the bowl.

"Anything happening?" Boss asked.

I shook my head and kept eating.

"Something's happening! Something's happening!" Dumhead yelled as he jumped up and down.

Boss and Louie grabbed me and started to pull me toward the john.

"No, no, no, it's happening! It's happening to me!" Dumbhead yelled.

Boss dropped me and took a swing at Dumhead as he ran to the most popular room in the house.

Then, again they started to feed me.

"Is it beginning to happen?" Boss asked.

"Stop questioning me! All of you are driving me crazy. If you keep asking me, it won't happen. If I can't, I won't. If I can I will."

"Yea, when he feels like it, it'll feel like it." Louie analyzed.

"How long after a meal before he feels like it?" Boss asked Sandra.

"Every day, it's different. Once, he couldn't do it for days, and we thought he would never do it again, but he did."

"Everybody got to go forever. We don't stop goin till we die." Louie said.

"You know a lot, Louie. I got to see what's in the things called books." Dumbhead said.

Sandra continued. "One time we thought Tony was dying because he wasn't even able to---"

"Sandra!" I yelled.

"I'm not saying anything wrong. I'm only telling them--" "Be quiet!" I insisted.

She started to cry. "It isn't my fault we're in this mess!"

"Oh, I suppose it's my fault. Maybe it's you and your mother's fault pushing me to your brother, the great doctor. He is the cause of all this!"

"OK, OK." Boss hollered. "We're not here to listen to you two fight. You, Tony, are here to perform. Go sit on the john so you can—"

"Perform! He's gonna perform on the john! He's gonna perform on the john!"

Dumbhead sang as he laughed and laughed until Boss kicked him in the rear and told him to put me on my throne. They kept the door open and watched me while Boss smoked his smelly cigar, and we all choked on the fumes.

"You better get used to this smell, Tony boy, cause I'm waiting patiently to get used to yours!"

"Tony's overwrought. He's very nervous that's why he can't do anything." Sandra said.

"You want maybe I should sing to him?" Dumbhead asked. "I was a good singer in my church. Maybe then he'll perform on the john."

"It might help dumbhead. I sang to him at home one night. Remember Tony? We were in bed and—"

Boss stood up.

"Singing ain't gonna help but maybe if I put a bullet through Sandra that would help."

Sandra screamed. "Tony, if you love me, do it! Do it for me, Tony, please."

"I want to do it. Please don't hurt my wife. My mother-in-law will kill me!"

"You said your mother-in-law was dead. We were gonna take here to cook."

"She is dead. I forgot."

"OK, OK, now perform that magic act of yours! We've been waitin long enough."

"How can I perform with this dam fly buzzing around in here spoiling my concentration?"

Dumbhead and Louie rolled-up newspapers and ran around trying to hit the fly until the phone rang.

"Stop the noise!" Boss yelled. "I can't hear anything!"

He went to another room to talk on his cell phone. When he came back, he said,

"That was, the man. He is very, very unhappy. He's comin to see Tony. I don't know when but don't look forward to it because he is strictly business and his business is torture!"

Sandra and I looked at each other.

"I'm gonna let you both go to sleep now. Just dream about, The Man, and maybe tomorrow will be a better day for work."

Louie and Dumhead tied us to the beds and took turns guarding us through the night.

The next day, they tortured me with food while Sandra watched the T.V. news about our kidnap.

"They are cruising the Queens Midtown Tunnel looking for us!" Sandra said.

"We ain't near that tunnel."

"Why are you telling her that?" Boss yelled at Dumbhead.

"She doesn't have any one to tell, Boss."

"The Man gets very angry when we tell anything. Remember, any more info, and I'll blow both your fucking hearts out!"

"OK, Boss." They chimed in unison.

I couldn't sleep. I kept trying to think of ways to escape. Besides, I was hot and dirty.

We hadn't washed since we came here three nights ago, and my stomach kept growling and giving me pain.

Sandra couldn't sleep either. I watched her head move from side and side across the room. We weren't close enough to talk, so I continued thinking.

It sounded like Boss was afraid of, The Man. I had read about terrorist operations and how they tortured people. We were in big trouble. We had to escape!

There was a very small window in the bathroom, and if I was left alone for a few minutes, I could possibly break the glass and yell for help. Boss said no one was around to hear us, but maybe he lied.

The only other possibility was the telephone. I had to try something! They wouldn't kill me unless they had orders to do it, but they could harm Sandra. I kept planning ways to escape until I finally dozed off.

The next morning, Boss scared Sandra.

"You better remember, girl, what it takes to make your guy do this thing, because you're in a head lot of trouble with The Man. We gotta follow his orders or our lives are at stake, so think about it, girl, think about it!"

"He needs chocolate!"

"Now he needs chocolate?"

"Yes, I remember Tony ate lots of my mother's homemade fudge, and he produced some wonderful things."

"Maybe we should kidnap the Mother. She'll make the fuckin fudge. Then he'll make us fuckin rich! Louie yelled.

"I told you she's dead!" I said.

"Ain't she the one who put a tent on your lawn?" Louie asked. "I have seen her on television! The Mother's alive! He's lyin!" Boss turned colors. He was enraged.

"My husband doesn't lie! He just meant she's brain dead. She has Alzheimer's. She can't remember anything. Not ever her fudge recipe."

"My wife is right. My Mother-in-law is a sad, sad case. Been brain dead for years. It was someone else's idea to pitch a tent on our lawn. She can't think for herself."

"Forget the Mother. Go get Tony chocolates, Dumbhead!"

"What kind of chocolates? The kind with nuts? A nut bar?"

"You're a nut bar!" Boss yelled. "Chocolate is chocolate!"

"No, no, no," Sandra interrupted. "Not every chocolate is the same. You have to find one with caramel or nuts or coconut. It definitely has to be brown. Not white or very dark chocolate because dark chocolate works in reverse on him. Also, see if you can find fudge. Fudge works great for Tony."

"Go, go get the damn chocolate! Here are two hundred dollars. Get boxes with all kinds of chocolates. Go, get out of here!"

While Dumhead was gone, I began to feel gassy," Sandra, I fell sick."

"My husband needs to move around. He can't do his business if he doesn't exercise."

Boss untied me and let me walk around, but I couldn't go out of the room.

I eyed the telephone. If only one guy was here to watch me, maybe I could get to the phone. Now, how could I get Boss and Louie to leave?

"I'm in pain. My hemorrhoids are killing me. Someone's got to buy me suppositories!"

I cried.

"My husband is suffering. You've got to get him suppositories!"

"I'll go, Boss. The drugstores are around the corner so I can walk." Louie said.

My plan sounded like it could work, so I continued to groan and moan.

"Somebody's got to help me. I can't do anything until this pain goes away."

I lay down on the bed and waited for my change.

"We got suppositories in the refrigerator. I use them all the time. I don't go a place without my suppositories." Boss said as he handed them to me.

I walked into my throne room really upset. "How about a little privacy?"

"You better not shut the door. We want to keep an eye on you. We don't want you should get ideas about escaping from that little bathroom window."

Boss read my mind.

"Oh, my Tony wouldn't do that. We don't want any trouble."

"Let me close the door. I can only do business when I'm alone. No one ever watched me before. And don't worry about me going out the window because I would never leave my wife behind."

"Speaking of behinds, lady, your loverboy will never see yours again if he doesn't use his!"

"Tony, he threatened me!"

"You better not do anything to my wife, or the cops will make you suffer!"

"How are they gonna find us? They're gonna follow your scent?"

The door opened, and Dumbhead came in loaded with boxes of chocolates.

Suddenly I felt something. I must have had a strange look on my face because Boss, Dumbhead, Louie, and Sandra came over to me. Everyone was silent.

"I feel something."

"He feels something, Boss."

"I heard. I heard."

"It's a sign. It's a sign."

"Signs don't mean anything. I gotta see the merchandise."

"It's a good sign, a very good sign. I can tell when my Tony feels something. How do you feel, Tony?"

"I am burning up. I have heartburn real bad. I need Turns."

"We don't have Tums, and you ain't getting any Tums. Just do your thin!" Boss yelled.

Sandra gave Boss a dirty look.

"Pretend we're at home, Tony, and you're in your own beautiful sitting room. I'll help you. Just listen to me."

"How can I pretend we're at home? It's hot and sticky, and the air stinks!"

"Maybe we should open the window for him." Dumhead said.

"You open the window, and I'll beat the crap out of you! You mindless mother fucker." Boss yelled.

Sandra bent down in front of me and started to talk. "Now, close your eyes and relax, Tony. Take a deep, deep breath. Count backward from ten, slowly."

"Hey, she's gonna hypnotize him." Louie said.

"She doesn't know how. She ain't one of them hypnotizers."

"Count backward, Tony. Let's feel that wonderful sensation inside us. We want to let it all out. We want to let it go. We feel it beginning. Let's make the noises. Make the noises with me Tony, Agh, Agh, Agh, and push, push, push."

Sandra was really trying for us. She had her heart and soul in it. She was feeling the feeling. She was seeing it. She was smelling it. She was polluting the air with it., Now, if only she would do it for me!

I wanted to feel that feeling. I knew something could happen, but I had to make it happen, or they could, in a fit of anger, kill us both!

"So, what do you feel, Mr. Tony?"

"I feel it going south."

"We'll be rich!" Dumbhead yelled as he and Louie The Lip danced and talked outside the john.

"Remember in the Bible there was this Golden Calf? Now we got the golden ass!"

They didn't stop laughing until Boss yelled. "Shut up, you morons, or you'll have your last supper!"

There was silence while everyone waited and watched with bated breath.

"I'm afraid it's just gas." I said.

"Listen, you! I'm getting sick of only smelling gas! I'll give you one last chance to make your move! Bring him chocolates! Lots and lots of chocolates!"

Louie brought me a huge bowl filled with chocolates.

"Mamma Mia! You don't expect me to eat while I'm sitting on the john, do you? No one eats while sitting on the john!"

"It's sacrilegious!" Sandra yelled. "Strange things happen to people who eat while they do it!"

"Yeah!" Dumhead said. "Same strange things like if you masturbate. You can lose your hair or an ear can fall off or"

Boss went over to Dumhead and put his gun in his mouth. "You can lose your tongue too."

I remained where I was and are chocolates, chocolates with peanut butter, chocolates with cherries, chocolates with peppermint, chocolates with cream, silver bells, chocolate marshmallows, plain milk chocolates, M and M's and fudge, lots of fudge, while my jailor watched.

"Mother's on TV!" Sandra yelled from the other. "She says if the gangsters will take her to us, she will cook her golden miracle soup and it will make Tony do more than he's ever done before. But of course, Mother can't remember the recipe. She is brain dead. She has that Alzheimer's Disease."

"Hey, Mr. Tony's got a strange look on his face." Louie held his nose. "And there's a different stink in the air."

Boss ran to look at me. He was all smiling. "I think we got a gusher! He inhaled. It smells like the real thing!"

"Sorry, Boss, but that was my fart." Dumbhead said.

As Boss raised his hand to hit him, Dumhead ran away, and Boss ran after him through the rooms. Suddenly we heard gunshots.

"Don't shoot me, Boss! I'll do anything you want!"

A few minutes later, they came back. Dumhead went down on his knees in front of me.

"Please Mr. Tony, do it for me cause if you don't, boss says he's gonna get rid of me and then your wife!"

"Tony, you've got to exercise!" Sandra cried. "Remember what the doctor said? You've got to give your constipation inspiration. Go sideways, backward, and forwards. Dance. Do the twist. Do something!"

Boss went to talk on the phone while Louie and, Dumhead sang and exercised with me.

"Gotta give your constipation inspiration, constipation inspiration."

I did the twist. I put my hands on my hips, and I bent and touched the floor abruptly. I felt something.

"It's coming! It's happening! I have that feeling! Yes! Yes! Yes! This is it!"

They helped me to my seat while Sandra held my hand. "I love you, Tony. I knew you could do it."

"You never lost faith in me, Sandra. It was because of your belief in me that I am able to do it."

Sandra bent down, and we kissed. It was a long, wet, loving kiss. I will always remember that feeling because kissing in that position is like nothing I have ever experienced before.

Louie and Dumhead held hands and danced around singing. "Halleluiah, halleluiah.

It's the coming. It's the comin."

Boss came running in. "What's happened?"

"It's a gusher, Boss. He's doing it! See?"

"You morons! Get the special containers! It's going all over the place! You're throwing out money! Get the special containers! Go find them! Don't just stand there like nincompoops! Get the shovels and shovel them into those containers for The Man!"

Boss took me from the room while the poor nincompoops shoveled and complained.

"This stuff looks strange."

"I don't want to look."

"Just pretend they're hot dogs"

"They don't smell like hot dogs."

"Stop breathing through your nose and you won't smell anything."

"I'll never eat a hot dog again."

"This ain't so bad. Sometimes my dogs' doo-doo is worse. Just think of all the money we can get from this stuff."

Boss tied us up, then drumhead and Louie put the containers in the car and left to deliver them to The Man, who was waiting to take them to his laboratory.

"I gave you what you wanted. Now let us go." I told Boss. "Please." Sandra begged.

"Not so soon, my friends." He smiled as he drank his beer.

"We have become like one big happy family. Just consider yourselves on a vacation."

"If you don't let us go, Tony will never give you anything again! Tell him, Tony!"

Boss wasn't upset.

"Little lady, with the food we're gonna feed your Tony, he will never stop giving!"

Sandra didn't stop.

"The police will find us. The whole world is looking for us. The President of the United States is looking for us. He has invited us to live in the White House. We've been invited to all the countries all over the world! Everyone is out searching for us! Do you realize how important we are?"

"Sure, sure. I know. Tony boy is the CEO of Shit Incorporated, but you've taken so much money out of the company that we gotta fine you!"

Just then, the TV had special news broadcast from the President.

"Tony and Sandra Costello, wherever you are, the world is thinking of you. We are putting every effort into finding you. To all who are listening, we have raised the reward from five million dollars to twenty million dollars. If anyone has any information about Tony and Sandra Costello, contact us through any police station."

Boss immediately went over and shut off the TV. A few minutes later, Louie and Dumbhead came in.

"The Man says he told you our share of the money will be here in two days. Is that right?"

"Are you questioning me? I told you when I get my money you will get yours. Meanwhile, don't put on the TV!"

"Louie and I already heard about the twenty million dollar reward on the radio."

"Don't get any weird ideas about taking that reward of The Man will have your head!"

Sandra cried out.

"So let us go. You're going to be rich. You'll have plenty of money when The Man pays you. You can leave the country. No one will find you."

"But we have the Golden Goose, and he will continue to lay golden eggs, ha, ha, ha."

XIII

Another week has passed, and we are still prisoners. Sandra is feeling sick, and I'm constantly struggling with nausea because the gangsters are always pushing food down my throat. They wake me in the middle of the night to eat and go, eat and go. I keep their containers filled, their car busy, and their pockets stuffed. The money gives them the incentive to keep me a prisoner. I am nothing but a machine for them.

If it wasn't for Sandra, I don't know if I could go on. At night, she sits next to me, and washes my face, pats my head, and whispers to me how much she loves me. She doesn't blame me anymore because she knows I can't do anything about our situation. I must provide them with what they want in order to keep us alive.

I found out they bring my stuff to a Doc Manhamen. I accidentally saw a paper with his address which I memorized, in case we're lucky enough to be rescued.

I told Boss, I would try to double what I was doing now if he set Sandra free.

"You double it. Then we'll talk about Sandra." He told me." Boss, she has seen our faces.

They both saw our faces. How are you gonna set them free?" Louie asked.

"Does this mean we will be killed when you're through with us?"

"Didn't I tell you we were like family? Would I kill my own family? Do you think I'm a terrorist? I'm a businessman. That's why I'm called Boss."

"But if you were ordered to kill us, would you do it?"

"Don't piss me off. The Man takes care of the killings. I see him do killings.

Why are you so interested in being killed? You just keep doing your job, so you and your wife can stay alive."

It was a nightmare that didn't seem to have an end. I looked over at Sandra, sleeping on one of the filthy couches. She looked exhausted, laying there in the same robe and slippers she had been kidnapped in. My pajamas were dirty and smelled. How wonderful it would be to have a shower, soak in a tub and take a shave. Why does it take something bad to happen before we appreciate the little things in life?

I was thankful they had untied us, and we were allowed to feed ourselves and walk to and from the bathroom. They put extra locks on the door, but Boss always kept the keys in his pocket.

Louie and Dumhead slept as I tried to talk to Boss.

"You gotta let us go. I can give you a couple of million and you can disappear to another country, and no one will be able to find you. If you have plastic surgery on your face, no one will ever recognize you. You could even afford to change your fingerprints.

Imagine how well you could live on some island with a couple of million. You could have everything you ever wanted, a beautiful home, great clothes, lots of women, cars and"

"These days, a couple of million ain't anything! I read the papers. I read about the guys that took all those millions from the stockholders. They knew what they needed to live in real style. A couple million ain't anything" Boss said.

"So how much money would you want me to give you to let us go? Whatever you want, I'll get it for you."

"I could be happy with ten million, but The Man, he's not so easy to hide from. He's a mean one. His kind ain't never gonna let me disappear. His kind would find me and torture me for days. His kind pulls out tongues, pulls out fingers one by one, sets fire to hair, and pulls out toenails. They are like Nazis! Did you ever hear of the Nazies?"

"Sure, who hasn't? They were rotten! So tell me, how did you ever get mixed up with these killers?" Boss sat down next to me and lit up his cigar.

"I guess I wanted to make money the easy way. But it turns out it ain't so easy."

"You could turn over a new leaf if you let us go. You could become a different kind of person, someone your mother would be proud of."

"I would like to be able to do that. I'm sure my mama would like that, too. She always wanted I should go back to school. I wanted to be a clothes designer, a woman's clothes designer. You know, like that Gucci and that saint person that makes all the expensive clothes. I could have been a saint something."

Boss got up and walked around. He checked on Sandra and lowered the lights.

"You're a lucky guy, Tony boy. You got a loving wife, and you could have had a real future.

How did you get mixed up in your stinking business?"

"I had no control of it. It took over my life, and before I realized it was addicted, like you, to the money. But I help people. I don't do it just for myself."

"You're a good person, Tony, but you don't seem smart, like from the mind. You don't seem like one of the creative people either. But you sure are one genius of an asshole!"

As he laughed, I heard something overhead. It came closer and closer. There was no mistaking that sound. I knew it well. It was a helicopter.

Boss jumped up and pulled out his gun.

"Wake up, guys!"

A bright light shined through the window blinds. Spotlights lit up the rooms.

Someone was on a loudspeaker.

"This is the police. You are completely surrounded!" "We're over here!" Sandra screamed. "In here!"

Boss pointed his gun at her.

"Shut up, you dumb broad! You want I should shoot you now?" He turned to his two henchmen.

"Quick, you guys, shut all the lights and get ready. We gotta shoot our way out!"

Dumhead and Louie ran around shutting the lights then stooping near the windows with guns.

"Dumhead, Louie, tie Tony and the broad's feet!" They quickly tied us up then ran back to the windows.

"What's the game plan?" Louie asked.

"We don't want any blood-bath, Boss!" Dumhead yelled.

Before Boss could answer, a voice shouted through a loudspeaker.

"Let the hostages go, or we will throw tear gas!"

"What if they throw gas, Boss?" Louie asked.

"We won't be able to see!" Dumhead cried.

"They won't do it! They don't want to hurt our friends here. They're only talking!"

Again we heard the voice on the loudspeaker.

"Let the hostages go, or we will come in and get you!"

There was silence. No one made a sound. Then abruptly, there was a thump on the roof. A chopper had landed.

"How are we gonna get out of here, Boss?" Louie cried.

Boss peeked out the window, then opened it crack and yelled.

"Listen to me! I'm giving you one warning! You let us go with our hostages, or we will shoot them!"

"Tony, they will kill us!" Sandra held me tight.

"You'll get the electric chair if you kill us! Let us go, and you'll only be held for kidnapping. I'll even pay for a lawyer to defend you!" I yelled.

"Fuck off!"

"Boss, maybe you should listen."

"You fuck off, too.

"Make a deal with them." I yelled. "It's better than spending your life in jail."

Boss shouted out the window, "We give you five minutes to disappear so we can leave with our hostages, or we shoot them dead!"

It was very quiet. We held our breath and listened for an answer. It remained quiet.

Boss looked at his watch.

"Their time is almost up."

"What are you gonna do, Boss? Are you gonna shoot them in cold blood? You never said we were gonna do killins!"

"Louie's right, Boss. Let's make a deal!"

"Bite your tongue!"

"What's to lose? Make a deal." I said.

"I want to give up, Boss!" Louie cried out.

"Me, too." Dumhead said.

Just then, gas started to fill the air, and I was unable to see. I was coughing and choking and couldn't breathe.

I felt someone next to me.

"We're police. I'm putting a gas mask on you."

"How is my wife?" I gasped.

"She's fine. Someone is helping her."

I stopped choking and began to see. The officers untied us, and I grabbed Sandra's hand. The rooms were filled with policemen, army soldiers, reporters, and the wonderful dogs they used to follow my scent.

We were helped into a police car, and from the car window; we watched our choking kidnappers being pulled from the building, handcuffed, and led into a police wagon.

The police took us to their station, where they cleaned us up, and we signed statements about our kidnapping. I gave them the address I had memorized about the head of the operation, Doc Manhamen, the real boss!

Sandra called her mother, who rushed down with Milton. I was never so happy to see Vera in my life. We kissed and hugged, and then the secret service men drove us home where Hiram and Amelia were waiting;

"We were afraid we would never see you again." They cried as they squeezed us tight.

The next few weeks, the TV and newspapers were filled with our pictures. Calls came in from strangers, all our relatives, friends, people we met at the White House, and of course, the President. Our life was an open book.

It took us a while to get back to the abnormal lifestyle we usually led, and during that time, I did a lot of thinking.

I wanted to fill the bellies of the poor, and I wanted to help the world against terrorism and all the other things that my contributions made possible, but Sandra and I were suffering.

Being one of the rich and famous wasn't everything it was cracked up to be, at least from where I always sat. So when Sandra complained how unhappy she was and only wanted a little house with a picket fence and children, to her astonishment, I took her in my arms and said.

"I want you to be happy, Sandra. It's time we lived a more normal life, a private life, and it's time we had a family."

Even Vera and Milton were pleased to hear I was going to have the reversal operation, but everything had to be done secretly.

XIV

Early one morning, I was taken into the hospital, and Milton, with two other doctors, performed my reversal operation.

This medical miracle gives me the ability to have that thing I have read about all my life and never experienced. Sex!

This wonderful, glorious feeling is much more than I anticipated, much, much more!

Sandra told me it would be like fireworks exploding, but I'm shooting torpedoes!

My medium-sized, cigar-shaped, self-propelled, stiff projectile that launches from my body, and is designed to detonate on contact with or in the vicinity of my target, is working in overdrive! This is a problem. I love doing it too much. I want to do it all the time. I never want to stop. I thought it would be a similar feeling to when I produced, but its sooo different.

Sandra is very, very happy now that I can get her pregnant, and I do my part, morning, noon and night. Because of my overabundance of sexual energy, Sandra walks around the house exhausted with her eyes half-closed, but she doesn't give up.

The doctors say my body will eventually adapt to a more normal sex drive, and I should stop trying to make up for all the years I couldn't have sex.

I'm really not trying to do that, but I can't help thinking of all those years when my pastime was watching football. Now I can enjoy this magical sensation at the same time.

Three months have passed since my operation, and Sandra is panicky because she isn't pregnant, so today we are going to see Dr. Herring, a famous fertility doctor in Manhattan.

Hiram is driving, and two detectives are escorting us because the government feels we are still at risk. I am very upset because Sandra's Mother is also with us, even though I argued this was a very private matter.

We have finally arrived. Hiram is remaining in the car to keep watch, while one detective is staying in the hall outside the doctor's office, and the other is one is sitting next to me holding his gun in his pocket. Vera, dear Vera, is next to Sandra.

There is no one else here because it was prearranged, for our safety, that Dr. Herring would not have any other patients in his waiting rooms of offices when we came here.

"Such an office! Like Hollywood, it looks." Vera commented.

I looked around. A green marble, the water fountain was in the middle of this huge, black marble waiting room. Antique furniture was everywhere and enormous oil paintings hung on the walls.

"Such a doctor's office! Vera exclaimed. "An office like this my son doesn't have. This Herring must be charging a lot for telling how to do when to do, where to do. In my day, in the bed with the husband you go, inside he puts the thin and poop, pregnant you were."

I was about to comment on my Mother-in-laws' remedy when Dr. Herring's pretty receptionist rolled in a table with beverages. "Make yourselves comfortable. The doctor will see you in a few minutes," she said with a big smile.

I noticed her nice hips but quickly pulled my eyes back in. I had to stop thinking constantly about sex.

The detective outside kept opening the door.

"Everything OK in here?"

"Ok." The other guard told him.

I noticed each detective was now holding his gun where it could be seen. I hoped there wouldn't be any trouble.

Finally, a smiling nurse came to get us.

"I'm Nurse Tillie, and I'm very sorry for the delay. We planned ahead that you would be seen right away."

"You know my daughter; she is here because she is impregnated?" Vera announced.

"Mother, she knows why we are here!"

"I want only to make sure in the right office we are."

"Just come with me.: the nurse said.

Sandra and I followed Nurse Tillie to the examining room which had two examination tables. I turned around and saw Vera had followed us in.

I shook my head and poi9nted to the door.

"Maybe my daughter wants I should stay." Vera asked.

I walked over to Vera, took her hand, and led her out the door as Nurse Tillie continued.

"Dr. Herring works with the husband and wife at the same time. He is one of the few doctors who work this way, and it has been very successful. He has been in personal contact with the doctors who performed the reversal operation on you at Gramercy Hospital and has gone over all your medical files, Mr. Costello.

Now, if each of you will go into separate cubicles, disrobe completely, and put on your hospital gowns, the doctor will be in to see you."

Nurse Tillie handed us our gowns and left us alone.

"I don't understand why I have to be checked over again. I was checked and rechecked before, during, and after my operation." I said.

"It's for our child's benefit. Remember, everything we are doing is for our child!"

Sandra went into her little cubicle to disrobe, and I went into mine. As I pulled off my pants, he talked to me.

"We must do whatever this fertility doctor tells us to do if we want to have a baby. Tony."

"Why don't we just let nature take its course? It's only been three months, and look at all the fun we can have to make a baby. We don't need a doctor."

I put on my hospital gown and came back into the examining room.

"What do you think this doctor is going to say to us? Do you think he's going to tell us to have sex differently?" I asked Sandra as she came in.

"Maybe."

"Sandra, we have tried it in every position possible!"

"He could know another position we never dream of."

"Oh sure, maybe he will give me a diagram so I know I'm heading in the right direction."

"We've gone all through this, Tony. You agreed to come with me today and do whatever was needed to be done. Now stop arguing about it!"

"I'll do it. I said I would do it, so I'll do it." I lay down on the examining table.

"I just hope he doesn't find some reason why I can't become pregnant, Tony."

Before I could reassure her, the door opened, and a tall man with a black, curly mustache walked in.

"I'm Dr. Herring. I'm glad to meet you both." He said as he shook our hands.

You're Brother-in-law, Milton and I spoke at length. You've had a fascinating life, Tony, but the most interesting part is only the beginning. Children will be a bonus to the fascinating life you had. I know because I have eight of my own. But let's get down to business. I'm going to take a few tests, send them to the lab, and then we will talk in my office across the hall."

Dr. Herring's nurse shut off the lights and told us to watch the pictures on the movie screen. While we watched x rated movies, they did something to my penis so they could get my sperms.

"You won't miss these little buggers, Tony. We men have millions and millions of them waiting to become beautiful people."

Next, they check Sandra's tubes, canals and organs. Then Doctor Herring did a very strange thing. He took what looked like a feather duster, and touched all of Sandra's body with it.

"Reactions, I need to see if her reactions to touch are normal."

"Are my reactions normal, Doctor?" Sandra asked.

"As normal as a rabbit, and that's very good."

"Maybe you should use the feather duster on me at home, Tony." Sandra said.

Two hours later, we dressed and went to speak to the doctor in his private office. Vera was already there waiting for us. "So Tony, now how it works he showed you?"

"Mama, he only took tests. I just hope I can conceive." The door opened, and Dr. Herring came in. I introduced Vera, and as they shook hands, he said,

"It's quite unusual to have a Mother-in-law at these sessions, but I'm glad to meet the Mother of the bride."

"A long time a bride she is. Seven years it is. Maybe you know why a grandchild I don't have?"

"We will find out that answer when our test comes back from the laboratory. I am very, very successful with my patients, Mrs. Horwitz, so you don't have to worry. They are in the best of hands."

"From a long time ago, you should know the problem mine Sandra had. Always the dentist would say, 'Open wide,' but always mine Sandra, quickly the mouth she would shut."

"My dear Mrs. Horwitz, I think you are confused. I am not a dentist. I never wanted to become a dentist, and I never will be a dentist. I am not here to fix the teeth in your daughter's mouth.

"Mama, the doctor knows what he is doing."

"About her mouth now, I don't talk, only about her closing shut someplace else I am talking."

"My dear Mrs. Horwitz, I am a doctor, a specialist. I have been a fertility specialist for over twenty years, and in all those years, no one has every compared my work to a dentist!"

"Doctor, explaining I am trying, but fammisht (mixed up) about some things you are."

"I am mixed up? Me, you feel it is me that is mixed up, Mrs. Horowitz? Perhaps there is something you want to teach me. Perhaps there is something you feel I don't know."

He stared at Vera as he wiped the sweat from his angry, ego, deflated face.

"Mother, please let the doctor do the talking."

"Do you live with your children, Mrs. Horowitz?"

"With them, I live, but my own wing I have."

"You have a wing?"

"Only one. The other wing I get when to heaven I go."

"Mrs. Horwitz, would you mind leaving us alone for a few minutes? There are some very personal things that I would like to discuss privately with Sandra and Tony."

"Who would mind? Only I want I should help. If away you need I should go, I go.

Outside the door, I wait."

Vera picked up her little plump body from the chair and waddled out the door.

Once the door closed, the doctor walked around the room for a few minutes without saying anything. He seemed to be in deep thought, so we didn't interrupt.

"We may have another reason why you are not pregnant, Sandra, and that reason just walked out the door."

"Oh, no, doctor, my mother couldn't be the cause!"

"Stress, stress, my dear. Indirectly, the stress she causes could make a newborn turn around and go back in the womb."

The doctor wiped his face again.

"Look how your Mother has upset me and I don't ever, ever get upset!"

The doctor sat down.

"I can't tell my mother to move out. I won't do it!"

"Even for the sake of having a child? You have to decide which comes first, the Mother or the egg! Because of stress, the subconscious part of your mind is telling your body that you don't want anything, you are depressed, and you don't even want to become pregnant!"

"But I want to have a baby! Everyone knows I want a baby. One of the main reasons Tony had the operation was because I wanted a child! There must be other things we can do, Doctor. Please make some suggestions."

"Well, you can just go home and keep trying. With Tony's, Pulsating, throbbing sex drive who knows what can happen. Don't hold back, Tony. Keep that drive alive!"

"Oh, he doesn't hold back, Dr. Herring. In fact, that has become a real problem. Since Tony's operation, everything turns him on."

"Be more explicit, Sandra. Tell me what you mean in more detail."

"She means I tire her out."

"It's more than that doctor. I find it hard to discuss." Sandra said.

"Well, that is why I am here, Sandra. Nothing will surprise me. I've heard everything before, so go ahead."

"Well, the other night I was eating an ice cream cone---" And."

"Tony, kept staring at me eating the ice cream cone--- and --- Tony, kept staring at me eating the ice cream cone--- and --- he literally pulled me upstairs to bed and kept reading, Me Tarzan, you James."

"And", the Doctor asked.

"I can't have a lollipop in front of him anymore because that drives him sexually insane, too."

"Sandra, there's nothing wrong with these things helping your husband rise up to the occasion."

"But there's more. He can't control himself with other women."

"Do you mean he's unfaithful?"

"Yes!"

"Sandra! I was never unfaithful to you!" I said.

"Maybe not physically, but mentally you were unfaithful. Whenever there is another woman around, you're unfaithful!

I just saw it when the doctor's receptionist came in. He even gets that look with our little old cook, Amelia!

My husband is always horny! He has become a man with a penis for a brain!"

"Sandra!" I yelled.

"Don't get excited. Calm down, both of you."

Dr. Herring looked at us while he curled his mustache.

"Your difficulties are because of the past five years when Tony was unable to function.

During that time, Sandra, you could be very sure that Tony was not thinking of sex or feeling sexually inclined."

"She was jealous then, too"

"I was not!"

"What about our house party? Remember your girlfriend, Iris, from school?"

"That was completely different!" Sandra exclaimed.

The doctor continued. "Now, since your husband's operation, he is a new man. He has sexual desires like other men but his body hasn't fully adjusted yet.

You, Sandra, also have to adjust because Tony may look at the other women until he dies."

"You mean I have to wait until he's dead to trust him?"

"Sandra, you have to understand the male libido. A man can get sexually aroused when there is nothing around to cause it. This feeling can come upon us when we sit in a chair and are alone. Sexual desire is an appetite.

"Tony is always hungry."

"He can't help it, Sandra. It's his hormones, specifically, it's his testosterone."

"I admit it. I constantly desire sex, even after an orgasm." I said.

"I do not advise that Tony's sexual state be changed by drugs at this time. If, after you become pregnant and have a child, Tony, is still hyperactive sexually, then I will suggest the right specialist who will give him a specific kind of treatment."

"So, doctor, I don't need to put a saddle on my horse."

"Definitely not, Tony. And Sandra, you should not hold back any waves of passion either. Here, take this special basal body thermometer to detect the rise in temperature, which shows you are ovulating and can conceive." He handed Sandra the thermometer and suggested we pick up some sexy magazines and watch some X-rated movies. "Don't be afraid to be a little kinky. Be explicit to each other. Express your desires and make this pleasurable experience of conceiving your first child one to remember.

Enjoy yourselves now, before you have that little angel who will take over your lives and give you in return: responsibilities, expenses, guilt trips, and no time for sex."

"You don't sound very encouraging, Doctor."

"Don't get the wrong idea. I love children, and the negative aspects are outweighed by the realization that you have brought your own little miracle into the world."

Just then, there was a knock on the door, and the voice of my Mother-in-law penetrated the air.

"It's okay I come in?"

"Yes, Mrs. Horowitz, come in."

"Doctor, if by chance, we are unable to have a child using the usual procedures, what can we do then?" Sandra asked.

"There is another way. I have worked for many years on a process different from any others, and have achieved great success. My discovery is an alternative to sex."

"From something else, never it could happen!" Vera said.

My Mother-in-law had spoken.

"Mrs. Horowitz, if you are a fertility specialist, I would like to know because then we could compare notes!"

He looked angrily at Vera, who thankfully kept her mouth shut and let him continue.

"This special method of mine creates a genetic duplicate of an individual organism. With this technique of mine and my degree of expertise, I can stimulate a single cell and create an identical child from one of you without any sex involved."

"My grandchild, an alien it will be!"

"Doctor, my husband and I would never go along with this. I'm amazed at your suggesting it!"

"My dear girl, what I have done is amazing! The scientific world is amazed at what I have accomplished. I am written up in every medical journal, in Who's Who and all over the world!"

"This isn't what we want, doctor." I said.

"This child would not be some monster. This child would just be a copy of one of you.

"Real it wouldn't be!" Vera said

"I have eight little ones at home, and they seem mighty real to me!"

"Eight little monsters, I can't believe." Vera said.

"My children are not monsters, Madam! They are made in my image!"

"I know nobody wants a mouth I should open, but I want to be a grandmother to a real child before too old I get." Sandra kissed her Mother.

"I'm so glad you feel this way, Mama. I really thought you just wanted Tony to keep working."

"No, already enough money he has. Now, home-like before he can stay and like my Perry Como, 'Oh, Sole A Mio', he can sing."

"No, Mama, he will sing like my Dino, 'Oh, Sole A Mio'."

"Maybe I will fool you both and sing a song I've been practicing called, 'Harva Negilla'"

Dr. Herring stoop up and with an angry look on his face said, "I don't really care I you sing, or if you don't sing, or when you sing, or what you sing, because I don't have time for this! I am a very busy medical doctor with a very busy medical practice!"

"Practicing you should keep doing. Maybe one day perfect you will make!" Vera said.

Doctor Herring ran out the door.

XV

It is almost a year since my reversal operation, and we have been very busy trying to make a baby. We have sex in the bathtub, in the pool, on the floor, in the car, on my desk, on our sing, in the attic, on our tennis court, on our trampoline, which I highly recommend, and wherever and whenever we are alone.

Everyone in our home, including our guards, knows hen Sandra ovulates, thanks to my Mother-in-law. They also know that she takes a pregnancy test with a dipstick, thanks to my Mother-in-law.

When it is Sandra's time of the moth to conceive, everyone questions us with their eyes, but my Mother-in-law doesn't use her eyes, only her mouth.

"So?"

"Mother, I will tell you when it happens!"

Then one morning, Sandra yelled to me from our bathroom. "Tony, come quick!"

I rushed in, afraid something happened, and it did! Sandra was standing in the middle of our bathroom, naked and smiling at the dipstick.

We kissed, hugged, yelled, danced, put on robes, and dashed out of our bedroom and down the staircase.

Everyone heard us and gathered at the foot of the stairs. Sandra and I took bows, and they applauded.

During the next few months, Sandra became pregnant. She had an ultrasound test, and we learned we were going to have twin boys. No thanks to Dr. Herring, who said he found us both sterile, and the only way we could have a child is if he cloned one.

Vera is thrilled and hovers over Sandra every minute. She won't let her move for fear she will exert herself. She insists on cooking everything Sandra eats while poor Amelia sits, watches, and smells the onions.

Sandra hired her favorite decorator, Tito, to do our babies' rooms. Tito is so thrilled about the twins you would think they were his sons about to be born. He dances through our home with his tiny, artist brush painting cherubs and angels on my sons' walls and ceilings. He thinks he is Michelangelo, but with today's prices.

"This is not the Sistine Chapel! I want ships, dogs, and cars on my boys' walls! I want real boys' rooms!" I told Tito.

"My dear man, you provoke me."

"I intend to provoke you until you change these rooms. I happen to be the guy who pays you!"

He continued painting the angel.

"I never talk money. I only paint. I am an artist. Artists don't speak of money. Go see my assistant."

When I complained to Sandra about the two bedrooms, she said to discuss it with the famous and very popular child expert she hired to handle all her problems before, during, and after she gives birth. She told me to be very careful what I say to him and how I talk to him because he could drop us and go to someone else.

"I don't what to speak to any experts. I want to discuss it with you!"

"I must not be upset. It will affect our child. You are upsetting my hormones! You are making me crazy. Go away! Go, go, go!"

She ran screaming into the other room. Those pregnancy hormones were killers!

They attacked husbands without any reason.

Amelia gave me the phone number of the child expert who instructed me to give my wife whatever she wants while she is pregnant, so our children will come out happy little fellows.

I asked him how many kids he had and learned he didn't have any and was never married.

"How did you become a child expert?" I asked.

"I took a course and put my name in the Yellow Pages."

"How much are we being charged?"

"I have been charging you four-hundred dollars an hour, twice a week, and I only work over the telephone. Don't you remember signing my agreement?"

"I'm not sure. Could you refresh my memory about what it said?"

"I certainly can. You hired me for the next five years. It says on the agreement, 'I am not responsible for any irregular behavior of a child. I am not responsible for a child's diaper problems, thumb sucking problems, eating or sleeping problems, or any school problems. I am not responsible for a child's swearing, stealing, hitting other people, or breaking things. I am not responsible for a child's swearing, stealing, hitting other people, or breaking things. I am not responsible for a child's giving, taking, or selling drugs. If a child has any mental, physical or emotional problems, I am not responsible. If a child runs away from home, or the mother or father leave home or divorce, I am not responsible for the child's attitude.

I couldn't believe my ears. I wasn't going to let this phony help raise my kids! I realized I couldn't upset Sandra now because her hormones would get me. I had to make the best of it and wait until after our children are born.

Meanwhile, we have been advised, in order to ensure the safety of our sons, and ourselves, that I must inform the public about my reversal operation and what it means.

So today, Sunday, the twenty-fourth of September, at high noon, the front lawn of our city hall is filled with: friends, relatives, interested citizens, television cameras, newsmen, and some government officials who are here to substantiate what I say.

Even though we are guarded by the police, the National Guard, CIA, and secret servicemen, we are all very nervous about this interview. We were warned that some people will not believe me and some people will be angry that I had the operation.

The United States Government has been very understanding and was agreeable about my operation. They are also very thankful for my past financial help and will continue to guard us because they feel we are still in danger.

As we sit here in front of the cameras, people are applauding but others are booing. A government official introduces me, I stand up, and he hands me the microphone.

"For the last two years, my family and I have lived with fear. They fear that we would be kidnapped, tortured, or killed. When this fear became a reality, it helped me make a decision.

I am sad to inform the public that for safety reasons, I had to have what is called a reversal operation, which permanently took away my ability to physically create wealth."

There was a great deal of booing from the audience so I stopped talking until they quieted down.

"I am very unhappy that I will not be able to give those large donations anymore to the millions of people everywhere, who need it so badly."

The booing from people continued, and some yelled out dirty names. I noticed many of them were taken away by officers.

"For two years, I tried to be all things to all people. I tried to do what I could for my country, and I will continue to try in a more normal capacity.

For the first time in my life, I am able to live the life that most people take for granted.

I am very grateful that I could be given this permanent reversal operation which makes it possible for me to be a real husband to my wife and a good father to children. I never thought I could have."

Again, many people applauded, while others yelled,

"You don't care about your country!"

"You only care about yourself!"

"You made your money. Now you're running away!"

It bothered me that people who had normal lives didn't want to accept my wanting the same thing. I was about to speak again and try to explain how I felt, but Milton whispered to me that it wouldn't help.

A politician from the local area shook my hand, then turned and handed Sandra the microphone. She smiled at me and began to speak.

"Life often makes us wade through a lot of mud so we can appreciate the beauty in a blade of grass. My Tony is more than that blade of grass to me. He is strong like a blade of steel. But, unlike steel, he is warm, kind, and loving. I am so very, very lucky to be married to this wonderful man."

Sandra kissed me right there on national T.V. big belly, hormones and all.

John MacCormick, the mayor, shook our hands.

"What a beautiful couple! And now let us hear from the Mother-in-law."

Everyone applauded and whistled for Vera. They remembered her from the tent.

Vera stood up very straight. "Unlike my usual self, from happiness, I know to speak.

My children are safe, and so thankful I am. So filled with amore I am."

Everyone yelled, whistled, and applauded. The public really liked her. Maybe she should run for office." I thought.

Finally, the most important speaker, and the real reason for this public gathering, safety for my family, was about to be introduced.

Milton stepped forward, and the government official from Washington introduced him.

"Dr. Milton Horowitz, the world is waiting to ask you one question. Professionally speaking, do you know if Tony's sons, who will inherit their father's genes, will inherit the ability their father had before his operation?"

Milton waited for a moment and then answered.

"This cannot be inherited. This ability cannot be inherited because it is not from the genes! The most brilliant doctors in the country have attested to this!"

The cameras flashed, and the reporters ran off to get their stories in before the deadline. The television session was over. Some of the crowd was in a jubilant mood and threw balloons up in the air, while others looked angry and disbelieving.

Now, when our boys are born, hopefully, they will be considered average human beings.

Thanks to Milton, little Max, and little Harry, will be safe because only Milton, the other doctors, and myself know the truth about my son's inheritance.